Alice in Rapture,
Sort of

Phyllis Reynolds Naylor

Alice in Rapture, Sort of

A Yearling Book

Published by
Bantam Doubleday Dell Books for Young Readers
a division of
Bantam Doubleday Dell Publishing Group, Inc.
1540 Broadway
New York, New York 10036

ISBN: 0-440-40462-2

Reprinted by arrangement with Macmillan Publishing Company, on behalf of Atheneum

Printed in the United States of America

June 1991

10   9   8   7   6   5   4

OPM

To Maureen Hayes, my special friend

Contents

1
Patrick and Me

I HAD JUST drunk my orange juice and was waiting for my toast to pop when Dad said, "Well, the summer of the first boyfriend!"

It sounded Wonderful and Sad and Magnificent somehow, like "The winter of our discontent," or "The spring of our desire," or "The autumn of our hopes and dreams." What he was really talking about, of course, was Patrick and me.

"I don't know if I can stand it," said Lester, my nineteen-year-old brother, who had a small piece of scrambled egg stuck in his mustache.

"You don't have to stand it," I told him. "You could always move out."

He ignored me, as he usually does. "I mean," he went on, talking to Dad, "how many times can I come home and find Alice and her boyfriend eating melted chocolate-covered cherries with a spoon?"

Just for that, I decided not to tell Lester about the scrambled egg. I hoped he would go all day with it there in his mustache and that he would meet the woman he wanted to marry, but all she'd be looking at was that little piece of yellow below his left nostril. Lester, though, was going with a new girl named Crystal Harkins, who played the clarinet, so maybe he'd already found the woman he wanted to marry, and the scrambled egg wouldn't matter.

Dad told me once that people only remember the stupid things that happen to themselves—that everyone else forgets almost as soon as they're over. Lester has a mind like an elephant, though. He'll remember those chocolate-covered cherries as long as he lives, mainly because Patrick and I had just dropped one on the porch and were deciding whether or not to eat it, when Lester came home and saw us.

It was only last week when that happened. And it was the first time Patrick ever kissed me. So the Summer of the First Boyfriend—the first *real* boyfriend— stretched out before me like a roller coaster. I didn't want to get off, but I was terrified of what was over the next hill.

My toast popped up. I buttered both sides, then drenched them in cinnamon and sugar.

"Have a little toast with your sugar," Dad said.

"I can't even stand looking at the way she eats!" Lester moaned.

"Look who's talking," I retorted.

Lester's on a "carb kick," as he calls it. He's into weight lifting and he gorges on carbohydrates. For breakfast he eats a stack of toaster waffles slathered with syrup, then toast, then cereal sprinkled with granola. He waits exactly forty minutes before he goes down to the basement and works out on his bench press. The whole basement smells like Lester's armpits.

I wonder what we'd be eating for breakfast if I had a mother. Homemade biscuits, I'll bet. French toast sprinkled with powdered sugar. Oatmeal, even.

I told Dad once that my earliest memory was of me sitting at the breakfast table with Mama, eating oatmeal.

"That was your aunt *Sally,* Al," Dad said. He always gets upset when I confuse Aunt Sally with Mama. "Your mother never made oatmeal in her life."

Mama died when I was five. I can only remember about one year out of those five, and a lot of what I remember is wrong. Scratch the oatmeal.

After breakfast, Dad went to work at the Melody Inn. It's one of a chain of music stores, and Dad's the manager of this one. Lester waited his forty minutes, then went downstairs to work out. When he finally showered and left the house for his summer job selling Maytag washing machines, I curled up on the sofa and thought about summer.

"Are you sure you trust Patrick and me in the house together?" I'd asked Dad only the day before.

"Shouldn't I?" Dad had said.

Parents love to do that—to answer a question with a question.

"I don't know," I told him.

"Well, if you feel uncomfortable, Al, you can always tell Patrick that I want the two of you out on the porch," he said.

I didn't know about that, either. If I told Patrick that Dad didn't want us alone in the house, it would sound as though he suspected Patrick of all sorts of things Patrick had never even thought of yet.

I guess it *was* the Summer of the First Boyfriend, not just for me but for Pamela Jones, too. She's the one with the blond hair so long that she sits on it, and she was going with Mark Stedmeister. You should have seen the way they kissed over by the grade school where we all hung around after dinner. She's not supposed to kiss until she's sixteen, though. Pamela's mom said if she ever caught her kissing, she'd cut off her hair. I asked Dad what hair had to do with kissing, and he said he hadn't the slightest idea.

Elizabeth, who lives across the street from me— beautiful Elizabeth with the thick, dark eyelashes— didn't have a boyfriend yet, but she liked some guy from St. Joseph's. So we were all sort of on the roller coaster together, Pamela and Elizabeth and I.

The phone rang and my heart bounced—the way you feel going down in an elevator. I knew it was Patrick. It had to be Patrick. He never calls in the afternoon because he's usually mowing lawns. In the morning, though, he's home waiting for the grass to dry.

The phone rang a second time.

Elizabeth says never answer the phone after the first ring because you'll sound too eager, and Pamela says if you wait for more than three rings, the boy will think you don't care. Pamela says that two-and-a-half rings are just about right.

I grabbed it after the second ring. It was Patrick.

"What are you doing?" he asked.

"Nothing much," I said. "What are *you* doing?"

"Talking to you," said Patrick. He always thinks of things like that to say.

I absolutely could not think of a single word to say next. The seconds ticked on. It was my turn! I had to think of something.

"Golda died," I blurted out finally.

"Who's Golda?"

"One of my guppies. The biggest one. I think she was pregnant again. I guess maybe I overfed her."

"Did you know that guppies give birth to live young?" Patrick asked me. "About fifty at a time?"

Patrick knows everything. He's lived in Spain and Germany and he can count to a hundred in Japanese and his family eats squid.

"Yes," I said. "I knew that." I'd been raising them, after all. I think he was a little surprised.

"Do you want me to come over?" Patrick asked.

"Do *you* want to?" I said.

"If you want me to," he answered.

"I do if you do," I told him. This was getting ridiculous.

"Okay, I'll come over," said Patrick, and hung up.

I rushed upstairs and brushed my teeth, changed my T-shirt, combed my hair, and put on a pair of sandals. Then I sat down on the couch again, mussed up my hair a little, pulled on my T-shirt to make it look baggy, and kicked off one sandal so it would look as though I hadn't even moved since he'd called.

I stuck both feet out in front of me. They were too big. My legs were too skinny. I looked like a starving prisoner of war, with my bony knees and big feet. I didn't have any hips to speak of, but I was beginning to get breasts, and I could have felt good about those if my lips weren't so thin and my hair wasn't so straight.

Patrick could have had any girlfriend he wanted out of the whole sixth grade last year, but he chose me. I'm sort of like Mrs. Plotkin, my sixth-grade teacher, I guess, who is ugly on the outside and beautiful on the inside and has this marvelous, adoring husband named Ned. Except I'm not really ugly. Just so terribly . . . *Alice.*

"How come you didn't choose Pamela or Elizabeth to go with?" I asked Patrick once.

"Because I like you," he said.

Life's weird.

I heard Patrick's bike squeaking to a stop outside. I heard it clunk against the house and then his footsteps on the porch. The doorbell rang.

"I guess we'd better sit out here," I said when I answered, and walked on over to the swing.

"How come?" asked Patrick.

" 'Cause Dad and Lester aren't home," I told him.

"Oh," said Patrick.

We sat side by side there on the porch, pushing against the floor with our feet, listening to the creak of the chains on the hooks above. After a while Patrick reached over and put his hand over mine on the swing between us.

I was thinking about French kissing, which is kissing with your mouths open. Pamela had never done it but she read about it in a magazine. I was wondering how many times you had to brush your teeth first before you French-kiss. You probably had to start planning it early in the morning and be careful what you ate all day so your mouth wouldn't taste like onions or anything. I'll bet if Pamela's mother ever caught her French kissing, she'd cut off her head.

"What are you thinking?" Patrick asked finally.

I felt I was on the roller coaster again, starting up the long hill to the top.

"What are *you* thinking?" I asked him.

"About that book of your brother's we were looking at last time," he said.

My shoulders slumped with relief. "I'll get it," I said, and jumped up.

It was called *Celebrity Yearbook,* with high school photos of famous people. You had to guess who they were, and the answers were in the back of the book.

"You mean *that's* Johnny Carson?" Patrick would say, and I'd laugh. Then we'd come to another picture and try to guess.

"Woody Allen!" we'd say, and laugh again.

Inside, on my way to the bookcase, I passed the porch window and saw Patrick take a breath mint out of his pocket and pop it in his mouth.

I stopped dead still on the rug. He was going to kiss me! The minute I went out there with that book, Patrick would kiss me. I ran upstairs and brushed my teeth all over again. I gargled with Scope. Then I got *Celebrity Yearbook* and went back out to the swing, my heart pounding like a tom-tom.

I sat down by Patrick and opened the book on my lap. The roller coaster started to climb. Patrick put one arm around my shoulder and leaned over as if he was looking at the pictures. I could smell the spearmint on his breath. One minute I was looking at a picture of Bill Cosby when he was eighteen and the next minute I was looking at Patrick's nose.

The kiss. The second kiss of the summer. Patrick's lips were cool and he pressed them a little harder against mine than he had the first time. He kept them there a little longer, too. I wondered if he was counting.

Then he sort of squeezed my shoulder with his hand, the kiss was over, the roller coaster was gliding to a stop, and I figured that now we could relax and enjoy the book. There are just certain things you're supposed to do when you're going with someone, and

I figured that Patrick kissed me first thing so we wouldn't have to worry about it all morning. I wondered how long you had to go with somebody before you stopped worrying. Before you stopped running inside to brush your teeth. Maybe by the time you were eighteen. The next time Lester brought Crystal Harkins over, I'd ask her.

2
Sleepover

THERE ARE some questions you can ask older girls, though, and some you can't. I couldn't just go up to Crystal Harkins and ask if she and Lester French-kissed or whether or not she brushed her teeth first. So Pamela and Elizabeth and I tried to figure things out for ourselves.

We did most of our talking on sleepovers at Pamela's or Elizabeth's house. I hadn't invited them to mine yet. I mean, usually there's a mother somewhere in the background making cocoa or lemonade, and I just didn't know about Dad or Lester trying to act like a mom. Lester, especially.

Elizabeth had a sleepover on Friday night. Elizabeth's the one whose First Communion picture is on her living room wall above the sofa. I suppose someday her wedding portrait will go up there beside it, and then the photos of all her kids. It must be really something to have a whole wall of a house reserved for you.

When we sleep at Elizabeth's house, we sleep in her bedroom, where there are twin beds with white ruffles at the bottom, and Mrs. Price puts up a cot along one wall. When we sleep at Pamela's, we sleep in the family room on a Hollywood bed, a trundle bed, and a cot. If the girls ever came to my house, we'd probably just have sleeping bags on the floor.

I was sitting on one ruffled bed with Elizabeth, watching Pamela paint her toenails. She was painting them cherry red and gluing little metallic butterflies in the center of each one. It made her toes look as though they were alive or something.

"You know what I heard?" Pamela said as she leaned way over and blew on her toes. "I heard that the very worst thing that can happen to you—next to having all your teeth knocked out in an accident or something—is to start seventh grade without a boyfriend. I'm so glad I've got Mark!"

Pamela always had the latest information about everything. Listening to Pamela was like having a map of a city without any roads on it. You knew where you were supposed to go, but you didn't know how to get there.

"Why?" I asked. Elizabeth never asks why. "I mean, why would it be so terrible if you didn't?"

"Because if you start junior high without a boyfriend, the guys will think you're a dog, and then you'll have to work twice as hard to be popular."

"A dog?" I said, wondering.

"A creep. A nerd," Pamela said, impatiently.

"Just because you don't have a *boyfriend*?"

"My cousin in New Jersey said."

That was the third time in a week that Pamela had given us the latest word from New Jersey. New Jersey was right next to New York, she reminded us, and her cousin knew absolutely the latest about everything. The first thing she told Pamela, and Pamela told us, was that a girl wasn't even *born* yet if she didn't have her ears pierced. The second thing she told Pamela was that a girl was absolutely *nothing* if she didn't own a leather skirt. And now, according to this New Jersey hot line, we all had to have steady boyfriends by the first week of September. I didn't own leather anything and didn't have holes in my ears, either, but I figured one out of three wasn't bad.

Actually, I was thinking about what it would be like to have my teeth knocked out in an accident, wondering if there wasn't something even worse than that, when I heard Elizabeth saying, *"You* don't have to worry about it, Alice. *I'm* the one who's not going steady. Just don't break up with Patrick till after school starts."

Somehow that made it seem pretty scary. "Why is it so important?" I asked.

Both of them looked at me as though I were still a baby on stewed prunes.

"For heaven's sake, Alice, there's got to be a boy in the background, that's all. What do *you* think when you see a guy letting a girl eat off his tray in the cafeteria and giving her his jacket when she's cold?" Pamela said.

"That she hasn't got any money?" I guessed.

Pamela rolled her eyes. "That he's her *slave*! That she's so ravishing he'd do *anything* for her. The other boys will simply go wild when they see how much Patrick cares about you and Mark cares about me, and from then on, all through high school, we'll never have to worry."

I had no idea it was so critical. It was like my whole life depended on what happened between Patrick and me the rest of the summer.

"It's just not fair," said Elizabeth. She plopped back on the bed and her thick black hair spread out in gorgeous curls on the pillow. "If I start going with a boy from St. Joseph's, no one at the junior high will know! It's not fair if you have a boyfriend and nobody knows."

"Maybe the girls could wear rubber bands around their wrists," I suggested helpfully.

Pamela paused with the nail polish in one hand and stared at me.

"In different colors," I said quickly.

Now both Elizabeth and Pamela were staring.

"I mean, girls who are already going with someone could wear blue bands and girls who are going with someone from another school could wear red bands. Then everyone would know."

"Girls who just broke up with somebody could wear yellow bands," said Pamela, getting interested.

"And girls who are going with someone but are just *about* to break up could wear purple," said Elizabeth.

Elizabeth's mother came into the room just then, carrying a big platter of fruit. The apples had been cut in rings and the orange slices had toothpicks in them and there were grapes and cherries around the edge, with the stems all pointing in the same direction. In the middle of all the fruit was a big heap of chocolate-chunk cookies from a bakery.

"A little something to eat," said Elizabeth's mother, and after she put the tray down, she came back with glasses of milk.

I wondered what kind of snack Dad would fix for my friends if I ever invited Elizabeth and Pamela for a sleepover. A box of Ritz crackers and some cheese, I guessed. Lester would probably just walk by the room and toss in a sack of pretzels. I decided to wait awhile before inviting Elizabeth and Pamela to my house for a sleepover.

After Mrs. Price had gone back to the kitchen, Elizabeth said, "My aunt Betsy told me that when she was in junior high school the girls used to put paper clips on the necklines of their blouses and the hems of their skirts, one paper clip for each time they'd been kissed."

Now it was my turn to stare.

"She said that girls used to come to school with the whole hem of their skirts lined in paper clips, and when they sat down it sounded like gravel going down a chute."

"What about girls who'd *never* been kissed?" I asked. I was thinking how I'd only been kissed by Patrick twice and how two paper clips on the hem of a skirt would look pretty skimpy.

"Alice, they all *faked* it!" Elizabeth said. *"Everyone* had paper clips."

"Then . . . what was the point?" I asked. I knew I asked stupid questions, but I had to know.

"To show that you were ready for it, that you wanted to be kissed, that you craved it with all your being!" Pamela told me, and we laughed.

"Maybe we should have a color for that," I said, thinking about the rubber bands again. "Maybe a girl who was desperate could wear all the colors at once."

Elizabeth thought that was a dumb idea.

We spent the first hour at Elizabeth's watching Pamela glue butterflies on her toenails, the second hour watching TV in the family room while Pamela talked to Mark on the phone. Elizabeth's mom had just brought in some egg rolls and set them on the coffee table when the phone rang again. Mrs. Price went back to the kitchen and answered there.

"Alice," she called. "It's for you."

"Me?" I got up and went out to the kitchen. Mrs. Price took her knitting into the living room.

"Hello?" I said. It was Patrick. "Patrick! How did

you know I was here?" I saw Pamela and Elizabeth smile at each other in the next room.

"Your brother told me," Patrick said. "How you doing?"

"Okay." I could feel my face getting red. I didn't know if I was pleased that he'd called me there or not. I wish that when boys called you on the phone they'd have something definite to say. I hate it during the silences.

"So what's happening?" Patrick wanted to know.

"Nothing much," I said. And then, because I couldn't think of anything else, I told him about the butterflies on Pamela's toenails. I heard Pamela giggle in the family room.

"That's the dumbest thing I ever heard," said Patrick.

"Yeah," I said.

Silence again. I was leaning against the kitchen wall, sliding down lower and lower until my feet were farther and farther from the wall, and when I was about to sit down, I'd straighten up and start sliding again.

"I got your note," said Patrick.

"What note?"

More silence. "Don't you even remember what you wrote?" Patrick asked me.

I stopped sliding. "I didn't send you any note."

"It's signed 'Alice,'" Patrick said. "It was in our mailbox this afternoon. It's a good thing I was the one who found it, too."

Suddenly I stood up as straight as a yardstick.

"What does it say?" I looked around the corner into the family room. The TV was still going but Pamela and Elizabeth had disappeared.

"You want me to read it to you?" Patrick asked.

I closed my eyes. "Yes."

"Just a minute," said Patrick. While he was looking for it, I took the phone and moved around into the other room, uncurling the cord behind me. I couldn't see Pamela or Elizabeth anywhere.

Patrick came back.

"My dearest," he read. My knees went weak. "I am going on a sleepover, but I wish it was with you."

I sat down on the floor. Hard.

Patrick read on: "I keep thinking of the last time we were together—your lips, your arms. I'm counting the hours when I will see you again. Your beloved Alice."

I felt as though I were choking. I sat there by the refrigerator in my shorts and T-shirt and thought about murder.

"Alice?" said Patrick. "Are you there?"

"I didn't write that note," I told him.

"It did seem pretty weird," he said.

I heard somebody giggle on the line, and then I knew that Elizabeth and Pamela were listening in.

"I think somebody's listening in," said Patrick.

"And I know who," I muttered. The giggling got louder and I heard a phone click. Pamela and Elizabeth were laughing back in the bedroom.

"Listen, Patrick, I'll talk to you tomorrow, okay?"

"Okay," he said. And then, softly, "Good-night, beloved Alice." I couldn't tell if he was laughing or not.

My neck was getting hot, my ears, my head. I was supposed to say something nice back, but my lips wouldn't move. In desperation, I wheeled around and pressed my finger down on the button. The dial tone came on. Slowly I hung up and stood with one hand on the receiver. Now he would think I was mad at him. Now we'd probably break up before I entered seventh grade and I'd have to wear all the rubber bands at once and boys would know I was desperate and I'd never get another date as long as I lived.

Pamela and Elizabeth stuck their heads around the corner.

"*Al*-ice," they chanted together. " How's *Pa*-trick?"

"Very funny," I said. I stormed into the family room and plopped down on the couch.

"Girls," Elizabeth's mother called, "if you're not going to watch TV, turn it off, would you?"

"We're watching," said Elizabeth.

We all sat and stared at the set and every so often Pamela and Elizabeth would break out laughing. Pamela laughed so hard she rolled off the couch. They went on back to the bedroom finally. After a while I turned off the set and went back, too.

"Can't you take a joke?" Pamela said.

"We're sorry," Elizabeth apologized, but as soon as she said it she started laughing again.

"Who wrote it?" I asked.

Elizabeth looked at Pamela.

"Oh, *he* knows you didn't write it," Pamela said. "We were just having fun."

"Listen," said Elizabeth. "You want to take baths with the Gardenia Deluxe bubble bath I got for my birthday? Pour two capfuls in the tub and you'll look like a movie star. I'll take pictures with my camera."

"Oh, no," I said. They'd take a picture before I got in the tub.

"We won't come in until you're ready," Elizabeth told me. "I *promise!*"

"I'll go first," said Pamela, and she took her pajamas into the bathroom and shut the door. I hoped her butterflies would fall off and her nail polish would chip and she'd have to wear braces until she was twenty-five.

"This stuff really works!" Pamela called a few minutes later. "Wow! Ready!"

Elizabeth took her flash camera, and we opened the bathroom door. Pamela had bubbles up to her shoulders. I had to smile.

Elizabeth took a couple of pictures—Pamela with one leg poking seductively out of the water, Pamela with one shoulder bare—and then it was Elizabeth's turn and we took pictures of her. By the time it was my turn, I wasn't mad anymore. If I was still going with Patrick on Valentine's Day, maybe I'd give him a picture of me in the Gardenia Deluxe bubble bath.

I kept the door locked until I was ready. When

everything was covered, I opened the door and Elizabeth took a picture. I had piled the bubbles on top of my head, too, like curls, and Pamela thought that was pretty funny. She said it looked like a wig.

We talked till one in the morning. Elizabeth dropped off to sleep first, then Pamela. At three, however, I was still wide awake, my eyes on the ceiling. Pamela gave little snorts in her sleep, but Elizabeth was as quiet as her First Communion picture.

I wondered if I'd ever be able to say that to a boy—". . . your lips, your arms." Without laughing, I mean. Or "beloved Patrick," the way he had said it to me. Look into his eyes and say it. I saw a movie once where a woman stared right into a man's eyes and said, "I *want* you! I *need* you!" and all kinds of things like that. And then they leaned closer and closer until they were breathing on each other and finally they kissed. I went out for popcorn and when I got back they were still kissing or starting all over again, I didn't know which.

I guess this is the kind of thing you talk about with your mother if you have a mother. Mrs. Price told me once that if I ever needed to, I could come to her. I can just imagine me asking Mrs. Price how you ever get to the place where you can say, "I *want* you! I *need* you!" to a boy without laughing. She'd tell Elizabeth and Elizabeth would tell Pamela and then it would be all over school. I decided I'd start a list of all the things I needed to know and call my aunt Sally in Chicago sometime.

3
Your Lips! Your Arms!

I T SEEMED as though Pamela, Elizabeth, and I spent the first two weeks of summer trying to figure out how we could get Tom Perona, the boy Elizabeth liked, to ask her to go with him. Steady, I mean.

We asked Mark Stedmeister to ask Tom what he thought of Elizabeth, but Mark forgot to do it. We asked Patrick to ask Tom to ask Elizabeth to go steady, but Patrick said, "If he wants to, he will." Everything is so simple to boys.

"Think, Alice!" Pamela would say to me at least twice a day, but I had other things to think about, too, that summer. My job, for one. Dad said he'd pay me three dollars an hour if I'd help out at the Melody Inn on Saturday mornings. It sells instruments and sheet music and has glass cubicles on the balcony where instructors give music lessons.

I always wore my best jeans when I went to Dad's store, a T-shirt that said HAPPY BIRTHDAY, BEETHOVEN, and sometimes my charm bracelet with the dangling silver-plated flutes and violins and trombones.

The weird thing is that I'm the only member of my family who can't carry a tune. Dad sings and plays the flute and the violin. Lester sings (howls, really) and plays the saxophone and the guitar. Dad made me take violin lessons when I was seven, but I lasted two months and gave up. I asked Les once what Mama was like, and he said she was tall and wore slacks and sang all the time around the house. I think what happened is that everyone else in the family got such a big dose of musical ability that there wasn't any left when it got to me.

For the first few years of my life I didn't even know I was a musical moron, but later on I'd sing "Happy Birthday" at parties and everyone would stare. I'd sing along at school, and the teacher would ask me to play the triangle instead. One of the great things about junior high school would be that there wouldn't be any music classes. Not for me, anyway. I couldn't have felt better if someone had told me I wouldn't have to go to the dentist again as long as I lived.

If somebody puts on a record of a song I know, I'll recognize it; I *like* music. But if you asked me to hum the melody, it would be like asking me to recite the Pledge of Allegiance in Chinese.

My job at the Melody Inn was to do about anything anyone asked me to do. If Janice Sherman, the assistant manager, got in a big order of sheet music, I'd read off the titles while she checked them in. If there were fingerprints and smudges on the glass walls of the practice cubicles, I'd take Windex and wash them off. I swept the walk out front and dusted all the pianos, vacuumed the carpet, and put fresh paper in the bathrooms. What I liked most, though, was helping Loretta Jenkins in the Gift Shoppe.

The Gift Shoppe, at the back of the store under the balcony, had all kinds of things you could give as presents to people who liked music and small items you might need for your instrument. There were trumpet cleaners and valve oil and guitar strings and dulcimer picks. There were notepads for musicians to put in their kitchens that said CHOPIN LISZT at the top, plaster busts of Brahms, Bach bracelets, Schumann T-shirts, and Tchaikovsky toothbrushes. There were music boxes that played "Clair de Lune" and ballerinas that turned slowly around on one toe to the theme song from *Doctor Zhivago.*

What I absolutely loved most, however, was the revolving wheel, a circular display case that, when you pressed a button, went slowly around and around so that you could see everything on the narrow shelves inside, mostly pins and bracelets and earrings and stuff. If you pressed the button again, the wheel would stop moving and you could look at some particular thing a long time.

It was one of my favorite jobs on Saturdays to see

that all the spaces in the revolving gift wheel were filled. If I had a hundred dollars, I would spend it all in the Gift Shoppe.

What I was looking for, actually, was a birthday present for Patrick. He was a couple of months younger than me, and I wanted to get him something special. I knew he played the drums. He had a six-piece Ludwig drum set, which Dad says is one of the very best drum sets made, but I couldn't buy him another drum unless I wanted to be in debt for the rest of my life.

"What about another pair of drumsticks?" Loretta Jenkins asked. "Drummers can always use those because they keep breaking."

I'd thought of that, but they seemed so ordinary.

"A pair of boxer shorts with Mick Jagger's picture on them?" she said. Loretta is about Lester's age, and her hair's a wild mass of curls. You take one look at Loretta and you know she says whatever comes to mind.

I blushed and shook my head. "I'll keep looking," I told her.

"Dad," I said later, dusting the grand piano where Dad was arranging a pair of white gloves and a conductor's baton, "what does a girl my age buy a boy Patrick's age for his birthday?"

"Hmmm," said Dad. "Here's where I wish you had a mother's guidance, Al. Candy, maybe? I just don't know. Ask Lester. Or better yet, call your aunt Sally."

"That's long distance," I reminded.

"It's okay. She'll know what to suggest."

When I got home at noon, Lester was just getting up. Every other Saturday, when Lester doesn't work, he has breakfast when we have lunch, lunch when we have dinner, and dinner around eleven o'clock at night. On those Saturdays, in fact, he has pizza for all three meals. Dad says Lester eats so much pizza he's going to start speaking Italian.

"Lester," I said, sitting down at the table across from him and making myself a peanut-butter-banana sandwich. "What does a girl my age buy a boy Patrick's age for his birthday?"

Lester groaned, as though a question like that could give him a headache. "It's too early in the morning, Al," he said, getting up and pouring some juice, his eyes only half open.

"It's afternoon."

"A straight razor and some shaving lotion," Lester said, his voice still groggy.

"Patrick doesn't shave yet."

"I know, but think how flattered he'd be."

"Think of something else," I told him.

"A six-pack of Coca-Cola."

"Something else."

"Couple pair of sweat socks and some Odor-Eaters."

"Something *romantic,* Lester, for heaven's sake!"

"Well, what do you expect at this hour of the day?" he said.

I went into the living room and dialed Aunt Sally in Chicago.

"Alice!" said Uncle Milt. "Sal, Alice is on the phone. Yes, *Alice,* from Silver Spring, Maryland."

"Alice!" said Aunt Sally. "What's wrong?"

That's the way my relatives are, see. The only time you call that they don't suspect something terrible is Christmas. And at Christmas, if you *don't* call, they suspect something terrible.

"Nothing's wrong. I was just wondering . . . uh . . . what a girl my age should give a boy for his birthday."

"Oh," said Aunt Sally, relieved. Then, "Oh!" again. "I assume that this isn't just any boy, but somebody special?"

"Yes," I told her.

"Well, dear, I'm so glad you called, because there are rules about things like that."

"There *are*?"

"There are only certain things you can give a boy before you're engaged, you know."

Engaged?

"You have to be awfully careful or your gift might suggest the wrong thing."

I had no idea it was so complicated.

"The only appropriate things to give a boy would be a book, a record, a wallet, or handkerchiefs," said Aunt Sally.

Every one of those suggestions fell like a brick on my head. Patrick already had a wallet, he didn't use handkerchiefs, and I couldn't buy him a book or record because I didn't know what he already had.

"Anything else?" I asked hopefully.

"Well, there are probably a few other things I've forgotten, but what you absolutely can*not* give a boy, unless you're engaged, is jewelry of any kind or any article of clothing that touches the skin directly."

I stood in stunned silence.

"A belt, now," Aunt Sally went on, "is perfectly proper because it's worn outside the trousers and doesn't touch his underwear."

My head was spinning.

"Just a minute, Alice," said Aunt Sally. "Carol just walked in. Maybe she'll have some ideas."

Carol was like an angel from heaven. Aunt Sally is my mother's older sister, and Carol is her daughter, my cousin.

"Sounds as though you're trying to buy a gift for a boy," Carol said, laughing.

"I'm so confused," I told her.

"Listen," she said. "Buy something fun. Go to one of those stores where they sell ski jackets and stuff for college men and see what sort of things they have on display near the cash register."

"Like what?"

"Like little cartons of chocolate-covered potato chips or miniature flashlights. You'll find something. You might even find some crazy boxer shorts with Mickey Mouse on them."

"Aunt Sally said . . ."

"I know. Nothing that touches the skin, right? Things have changed since she was a girl, Alice. Have fun."

Now that I had her on the phone, I wondered if I should ask how you know when you're ready to say "I *want* you! I *need* you!" to a boy. But with Aunt Sally there in the room with Carol, and Lester in the room next to me, I figured I'd better not ask that now. I wasn't about to say it to Patrick, anyway, birthday or not.

That afternoon at the mall, I found a little carton of chocolate-covered potato chips at Britches of Georgetown, just as Carol had said I would. I wanted to get at least one more thing for Patrick, though, and at the Melody Inn the next Saturday I found it—a little dollhouse-size three-piece drum set that had just come in. It looked as though it was made of ivory. GENUINE LUCITE, it said on a little gold tag. It was only $4.98 without my 10 percent discount.

When Patrick came by that evening, we sat out on the porch steps while he unwrapped his gifts.

"Hey!" he said, pleased, when he saw the chocolate-covered potato chips. "These are really great!" He offered one to me, and I let him have the rest. He ate them all before he opened the second present. There were oodles of tissue paper around it, because I didn't want the Lucite to get scratched.

"Wow!" he said. "Alice, this is really nice!" He turned the little drum set around and around in his hands. "I'll keep it on my dresser," he said. And then he leaned over and kissed me. It seemed so natural that I didn't even get flustered.

I sort of turned the tag around on the drum set so he'd be sure and notice, and when he didn't say anything, I said, "Genuine Lucite."

"Oh, yeah!" said Patrick. "Well, it's really nice, all right."

We walked around the neighborhood holding hands. Once, on a long stretch of sidewalk where thick trees blotted out the light from the streetlamps, Patrick put his hands on my shoulders and turned me around and kissed me. (That would make *four* paper clips to put on my dress!) This time it wasn't just a quick smack on the mouth, but a real kiss. He really put his arms around me. He really pulled me close. It was so romantic my legs felt as though they were melting. I could feel my heart pounding, pounding, beneath my checked shirt. *Your lips, your arms!*

I wondered if *this* was how you felt when you said, "I *want* you! I *need* you!" But I figured you had to go through a lot of kisses first before you ever told a boy something like that. I was really proud of myself that day: for choosing such nice gifts for Patrick; for not giggling or anything when he kissed me.

Patrick acts a lot older than his age. I guess it's because he's traveled so much and seen so many things. I wonder sometimes if he practiced kissing girls before me. Then I remember that first kiss on our porch with the chocolate-covered cherries and decide he didn't. The thing about Patrick is he doesn't get embarrassed easily. I get embarrassed about everything. I get embarrassed for getting embarrassed.

Sunday afternoon I sat down with Lester to watch "Wide World of Sports" on TV. Lester watched, actually. I was staring dreamily out of the window.

"You look like the cat that swallowed the canary," Lester said during a commercial.

"I am," I told him.

"You and Patrick get engaged or something?"

"Very funny," I said. "I happened to find the perfect birthday present for Patrick, that's what—a miniature drum set to put on his dresser."

"Sounds nice."

"It is. He really likes it."

The sailboat races came on again and Lester's eyes were glued to the set.

"Lester," I said, interrupting. "What's Lucite?"

Lester shrugged. "Some kind of plastic, I think."

I leaned back hard against the couch. Plastic? I gave Patrick a present with a little gold tag that said *genuine plastic*?

I called Elizabeth and Pamela. The nice thing about telling girlfriends what you've done is that it spreads the pain around. The way they moaned and wailed, it was as though we were all in it together.

The next time I called Aunt Sally in Chicago, I was going to add a new rule to her list: Never give a boy anything with a little gold tag that says LUCITE.

4
The Girl with the Corkscrew Curls

WE MADE UP our minds the day after that—
Pamela, Elizabeth, and I—that we would make Elizabeth so ravishing that the next time Tom Perona
looked at her, he'd just *have* to ask her to go with him.
Unless boys from St. Joseph's aren't supposed to look
at girls that way.

"What way?" Elizabeth asked as we brushed her
dark curly hair.

"*You* know," said Pamela. "With passion."

"Don't talk about that," said Elizabeth.

So we just brushed.

When we got through brushing her hair, though,
she looked about the same. Absolutely gorgeous.
We even put blush on her cheeks and gloss on her

lips and that hardly changed her a bit. Elizabeth is one of those girls who is simply born beautiful.

So we turned our attention to Pamela to see what lip gloss and blush would do for her. The fact is, however, that when you've got blond hair so long that you can sit on it, you don't need to think about your face at all.

Then Pamela and Elizabeth turned their attention to me and hardly knew where to begin. They brushed for about twenty minutes, but all it did was make my hair stand out away from my head as though I'd been hit by lightning.

"I don't know, Alice," Pamela said finally. "Maybe you need a haircut or something."

I hadn't had a haircut since I'd been to Chicago over spring vacation and my cousin cut it. I guess Pamela was right, because that evening Lester told me I was beginning to look like a sheepdog. But it wasn't until the next day when Dad said, "Al, we've got to do something about that hair," that I knew it was just too awful to ignore.

Lester was trying to read the paper on Tuesday before he went to work, but I wanted to try out a few ideas on him. First I piled my hair on top of my head and tied it with a ribbon, sort of like you'd wrap a perfume bottle for Christmas.

"Lester," I said, leaning in front of his newspaper. "Imagine how I'd look if all this hair up here was curly. What do you think?"

Lester leaned way back as though I were a wet

dog trying to crawl onto his lap. "Give me a break," he said.

I went back up to my bedroom, untied the ribbon, parted my hair on one side, and pulled it down over my eye, tucking the other half behind one ear.

"Is this any better?" I said, back downstairs again.

"You look like something out of a Charles Addams cartoon," Lester told me. "What's that woman's name? Morticia?"

It was Dad who had the idea. That night, when I told him I thought I'd look better with curls, curls like Elizabeth has—large, luscious curls that spread out over her pillow—he said, "Your mother used to get permanents. Why don't we make an appointment for you to get a permanent, Al?"

There was something about knowing I was going to fix my hair like my mom's that made me feel all soft and warm inside. Which is why, that very Saturday, I was sitting with a plastic cape around my shoulders in La Chic Salon, handing little white squares of paper to the beautician who was using them to wrap each curl around a roller until my whole head looked like a telephone switchboard. After that she poured a bottle of something that smelled like cat pee on my head, and then I had to sit under a dryer for fifteen minutes with a long roll of cotton around my face to keep the cat pee from trickling down into my eyes. When that was over the beautician rinsed the curls, poured on something else, rinsed my hair again, and finally took out the rollers.

"Don't wash your hair for seventy-two hours," she said as I left, curly headed, and all the way home I wondered what would happen if I did. I still smelled like a cat's litter box, but the beautician had said that would disappear in a few days.

I knew I still had the same face—I didn't look like Elizabeth or anything—but somehow I had thought the curls would look better than they did. They were tight and small.

"Give me a break," Lester said again when he got home from selling Maytags and saw me.

"It's like Mom used to wear her hair," I told him.

"On Mom it looked different," Lester said.

When Dad got home from the Melody Inn, I could tell by his eyes that the permanent hadn't turned out the way he'd thought it would, either.

"Look," I said, gulping. I picked up a curl with two fingers, pulled it out away from my head, and let go. It sprang right back against my scalp like a bedspring. The girl with the corkscrew curls. I felt like bawling.

As the evening went on, my hair got even worse. The curls seemed to be shrinking smaller and tighter. Patrick was out of town for the weekend with his parents, and I was glad because I knew that if he got close to me, he'd think a cat had sat on my head.

I went to bed early so I wouldn't have to think about the permanent, but when I woke the next morning, even my pillow smelled like cats. When I looked in the mirror, I couldn't believe it. I looked like a little old lady with curls stuck tight to her head. And sud-

denly the word *permanent* struck home. I remembered spilling some permanent ink on my jeans once
and it never did come out, not even with Clorox. Was
I going to look like this for the rest of my life? What
could be worse than starting seventh grade without a
boyfriend? Getting a permanent at the La Chic Salon,
that's what!

Patrick got home late Sunday night, so he called
me Monday morning and asked if he could come
over.

"I'm sort of sick, Patrick," I said.

"What's the matter?" he asked.

That's one thing about boys: They ask dumb
questions. What if I'd had diarrhea? Elizabeth said
once that if there's something embarrassing wrong
with you, you can always say you have the flu. I guess
the church doesn't consider that a lie or anything.

"I've got the flu," I told Patrick.

"What kind?" he asked. "Chest or stomach?"

Why do boys *do* that? How do you tell him it's flu
of the hair?

"I think it's in my head," I said finally.

"That's respiratory," said Patrick. "That can stop
up your ears and everything. Gee, I'm sorry, Alice. I
was hoping I could see you tonight."

"Yeah, my lucky day," I told him.

As soon as dinner was over, Dad went off to a
friend's house to play chamber music on his violin. It
was Lester's turn to do the dishes, and he was waiting
for his girlfriend, Crystal Harkins, to come over. I had

just taken a piece of Sara Lee chocolate cake upstairs to eat in my room when I heard the doorbell ring. I paused at the top of the stairs, the cake halfway to my mouth.

"Hey, Patrick!" I heard Lester say. "How you doing?"

I froze. I mean, it's like in a dream where you're standing on the railroad tracks and you see a train coming but you can't move.

"I was wondering how Alice is," Patrick said. "I just thought I'd come by and leave these here for her."

There was a three-second pause.

"Alice?" said Lester, as though he'd never heard of me before. "What's wrong with her?"

I closed my eyes and leaned against the wall.

"She's got the flu," said Patrick.

"She has?" I could almost hear the wheels turning in Lester's dull brain. "Oh! The flu! I guess she *doesn't* look so good today," he said finally.

I let out a sigh of relief and took a bite of the chocolate cake. As soon as Patrick left, I'd go down-stairs and see what he brought me.

"Maybe I could give her these myself," Patrick said.

I bolted from the wall and spit out the cake in my hand. *No!* I whispered, trying desperately to communicate with Lester by mental telepathy. *Say no, Lester. Please say no!*

"I don't see why not," Lester said. "Hey, Al! Patrick's coming up for a minute. Okay?"

I raced down the hall to the bathroom, shut the door, flushed the cake down the toilet, rinsed out my mouth, sprayed my head with room deodorizer, and wrapped a towel around my head like a turban. Why do boys *do* that! What if I didn't have any clothes on and Patrick was on his way up? Don't brothers ever think?

I opened the bathroom door and there was Patrick, clutching a bouquet of flowers. He stared. I walked slowly toward him, steadying myself with one hand and holding the towel with the other.

"Gosh, Alice, you look different," he said, following me back to my room.

My room! Patrick was coming into my room! I still had yesterday's underpants on the floor. I still had my training bra hanging on my chair. I had sneakers that smelled like sneakers on the rug. I hadn't made my bed, and there was still a half-eaten piece of pizza on my dresser.

As I walked into the room, I kicked both my underpants and my sneakers under the bed. I grabbed the bra and stuck it under my T-shirt. Then I sat down on the edge of the bed, holding the towel with one hand and the hidden bra with the other. I felt miserable.

"You look miserable," said Patrick, handing me the flowers. I took them with one hand and held them against my T-shirt so the bra wouldn't fall out.

"Thanks," I said.

"Why have you got that towel on your head?" Patrick wanted to know.

"Well . . . I've . . . uh . . . sort of got medicine on my head," I told him.

"Oh," said Patrick, and stared some more.

"I have to leave it on for another day. Thanks for the flowers," I said again, hoping he'd leave.

"They're from Mom's garden," said Patrick, and took a step closer.

No! I thought. *Don't try to kiss me, Patrick. Please don't try to kiss me!*

He took another step.

"I wouldn't want you to catch anything," I said. "I'll bet I'm contagious as anything."

"I don't care," said Patrick. He leaned over and gave me a light kiss on the cheek.

"Whew!" he said, straightening up again. "I sure hope that stuff on your head helps."

"It's awful, I know," I told him.

When Patrick left, I began to bawl. I went to the top of the stairs and screamed at Lester. By that time I was crying so hard I could hardly talk.

"I hope all your hair falls out and your teeth rot and your feet go flat!" I bellowed, sobbing. "How could you *do* that to me, Lester? I *hate* you!"

Lester came to the bottom of the stairs and looked up at me, his mouth hanging open.

"What the heck's wrong with you, Al?" he said. "What was I supposed to do? Send him back home? I didn't even know you were sick."

"I'm *not* sick!" I shrieked, and then, "I'm ugly! I'm

ruined! My room smells like dirty socks, and you let Patrick see me like this!"

"Hey, easy! Easy!" Lester said. "You think Patrick's never smelled feet before?"

But I rushed back into my room and threw myself on the bed. If ever I needed a mother, it was then.

At that precise moment, Crystal Harkins rang the bell, and Lester let her in. Before I knew it, I could hear Crystal and Lester talking in the hall outside my room and Lester saying how upset I was. He actually sounded sorry for me. I heard footsteps going away and I thought they had both gone back downstairs, but then I felt someone sit down on the edge of my bed.

I don't know how Lester does it, but with all his faults, he's had some really nice girlfriends. Crystal Harkins had sort of reddish hair, real short, and a big bosom. She was pretty in a friendly sort of way, which is the prettiest way you can be. She put one hand on my shoulder, and I just curled up there on the bed with my head against her leg. I'll bet my tears were soaking right through her jeans, but she didn't seem to care. The towel had fallen off my hair, and I knew that Crystal Harkins was seeing me at my worst.

"Looks like somebody had a permanent," Crystal said, and ran one hand through my hair. I didn't know how she could stand it.

"It's . . . it's . . . going to stay this way forever," I sobbed.

"Only until your hair grows out," Crystal said. "Permanents only last a few months."

I stopped crying. "It will be gone before I start junior high?"

"Most of it. But you may want another one by then."

"Hoo, boy, not me!"

"You wait and see. I'm going to make you beautiful," said Crystal.

Those are the six most wonderful words in the English language: *I'm going to make you beautiful.* I couldn't believe my ears.

Crystal took me into the bathroom and washed my hair at the sink. She said we didn't have to wait the full seventy-two hours if we did it very gently. Then she dried it with a towel and showed me how to take a circular brush, wrap it around a lock of hair, and hold it out away from my head while I dried it with the blower. Result: one big, beautiful, gorgeous curl, just like Elizabeth's. Crystal did half my head and let me do the rest. She said that for the next week, until my curls loosened up a bit, that's the way I could make myself beautiful. After that, for a few months, anyway, the curls would take care of themselves.

I just stared and stared in the mirror. I looked like one of those shampoo girls on TV.

You know what I did? I threw my arms around Crystal and hugged her. I wished that Lester would marry her and she would live with us always. I wanted to ask her how she felt about Lester. I wanted to ask how long you had to go with a boy before you stopped worrying about your breath and your hair and everything, but I just kept saying, "Thank you, Crystal, thank you!" I hugged her again and she hugged back.

I walked downstairs like a princess. Lester stared. I turned around slowly so he could see how beautiful I was from all sides.

"It looks great, Al!" he said. "Really!"

"I know," I told him.

When Patrick called later to see if I was any better, I thanked him again for the flowers and told him that I was feeling much, much, much better.

"Good," said Patrick.

5
Bad Mommies

WE'D GO WHOLE days in our house when it seemed as though Dad hardly worried about me at all. Then, all of a sudden, he'd ask a question or give me a look or something that let me know that The Summer of the First Boyfriend was making him a little bit nervous, too.

"What'd you do all day, Al?" he'd ask sometimes. And then, "Did Patrick come over?" And when he found out that Patrick came by almost every day, he began asking, "What'd you do today?" almost as soon as he got home from work.

At first, I acted smart about it. I'd say, "Well, I got up and walked in the bathroom and brushed my teeth, and then I went downstairs and made some toast and put butter on it, and . . ." It would take me five minutes just to get as far as lunch. But when I realized that Dad was really concerned about me, I'd tell him what he wanted to know—namely, what Patrick and I did together.

A lot of the time we just sat on the porch swing and talked (and kissed), but at least once a week we went to Mark Stedmeister's pool with Pamela. Once in a while Tom Perona would go up and down the street on his dirt bike, and then Elizabeth would come over and she and Patrick and I would sit on the steps watching Tom do wheelies and things on his bike. If it wasn't too hot, all six of us—Mark and Pamela, Elizabeth and Tom (even though they weren't officially going together), and Patrick and I—would take a basketball over to the grade school and play a few games, or if it *was* hot, we'd take a bus to Wheaton Plaza and spend a few hours there. Dad always liked to know the details: when I left, who I was with, when I got back, and what we did. Fathers get nervous unless they have all the details.

So, when Elizabeth, Pamela, and I started baby-sitting for the neighbors, Dad was happy to have me occupied. It's weird, though. Nobody ever asked us to baby-sit when we were in sixth grade. But now that we were going into seventh, it was as if people suddenly decided we could be trusted. And the third week of July, when Mrs. Benton, in the next block, decided to go back to work two afternoons a week and hired me to baby-sit Jimmy on Tuesdays and Thursdays, Dad was *really* pleased. Now he knew exactly where I was and what I was doing—two afternoons out of five, anyway.

I liked having a steady job, but I wasn't too sure about Jimmy. For one thing, most of the kids I had taken care of were babies, and they slept a lot. Cry, eat, wet, and sleep. But Jimmy Benton was three years old, and his mother had never left him with a sitter for very long.

The first Tuesday I was to start work, I told Dad I was a little scared. "What if he won't take a nap?" I wondered.

"You're clever enough to think of something," Dad told me.

"Try singing to him, Al," Lester said, over his waffles. "Tell him you won't stop singing unless he takes a nap. That'll shut him up quick."

I still had some of the books I used to like when I was small—*Little Bear's Visit* and *Goodnight, Moon* —so I took those with me when I left the house. When I reached the Bentons', I gave Jimmy a big smile, but he just put his hands over his eyes and wouldn't look at me.

"I'm afraid you might have some problems with him at first," Mrs. Benton told me. "I've tried to explain to him that I have a job now just like his daddy, but it's hard to know how much a three-year-old understands."

"We'll get along fine," I promised, but I wasn't sure. When Mrs. Benton bent down to kiss Jimmy good-bye, he hit her on the cheek.

"Bad Mommy," he said, and went into the other room to watch television.

Mrs. Benton looked as though she were going to cry.

"He'll be fine," I said again. "If there's any real problem, I'll call you."

But I was sure it was *not* going to be fine when, after Mrs. Benton left, I sat down by Jimmy and he kicked my leg. *Hard.*

I tried to show him where the little hand on the clock would be when his mother came home. Jimmy hit the clock. I built a tower for him with his blocks. He knocked it down. I told him I'd read to him if he'd sit beside me. He wouldn't come. When I picked up *Little Bear's Visit* and began reading aloud, he rushed me from across the room and butted his head against the book.

I really wanted to make the job work, because it was the first steady job I had had, outside of helping Dad at the Melody Inn. More than that, there was something about Jimmy Benton that made me *want* to like him, even though I couldn't think of any real reason why I should.

An hour into the job, though, I was worn out. I was bruised. Nothing I tried seemed to work. I saw a TV show once where a therapist did everything the child did to show that she accepted him just as he was. So I tried doing whatever Jimmy did. When he kicked his blocks across the floor, I kicked blocks. When he scrunched up his eyes and screeched, I screeched. He stared at me. When he sat down on the couch and banged his head against the back, so did I. Finally, he curled up at the end with his thumb in his mouth, looking very, very sad and small and lonely, and I decided right then that I liked Jimmy Benton, no matter what.

He kept on sucking his thumb and twisting a lock of hair around and around his finger. After a while he fell asleep, and even though Mrs. Benton had told me to put him in his room for a nap at two, I wasn't about to touch him for anything. While he was asleep, I straightened up the house a little, picked up all his toys, put out two graham crackers for his snack when he woke up, then sat down to read a magazine.

There were seven different shampoo ads in the magazine, and in every one of them the woman had curls just like mine. In every single picture, the woman had her head tipped back, and curls were falling down around her shoulders. In every picture there was a man in the background who looked as though he just couldn't wait to run his fingers through the woman's hair. And all the women were smiling, ignoring the man, as though women who used that kind of shampoo just had to get used to men moaning over them back in the trees.

I went over to the mirror by the front door and slowly tipped my head to see how far down my back my hair would come. I looked at the way the women in the magazines were smiling, and I practiced the same kind of smile in the mirror. The next time Patrick came over, I decided, I'd be standing on the porch waiting for him, leaning against a post, my head tipped just a little showing my long luxurious throat, and I would smile as he came up the steps and put his arms around me.

I stopped smiling suddenly. Back on the sofa, Jimmy was awake and watching.

"Snack time!" I sang out, and poured a glass of grape juice. I had hoped that when Jimmy woke up, he would feel better. Wrong. Jimmy felt worse.

"Alice poo-poo," he called me.

He picked up his grape juice, drank half of it, and poured the rest over his graham crackers.

That's it, I thought to myself. *Just stick it out till five o'clock and then you can quit this job.*

I cleaned up the mess without a word, washed Jimmy's hands and face, and then sat down on the floor and took all the toys out of the toy box, one at a time, talking to myself: "This is a fire engine. Wow! Look at that ladder!"

Jimmy grabbed the fire engine out of my hands.

"Here's a hospital!" I said, picking up a little Playskool building, with a Playskool doctor, nurse, and three little Playskool patients.

Jimmy grabbed the Playskool nurse. He put her in the fire engine and ran it pell mell along the rug. The Playskool nurse fell out and the fire engine backed up and ran right over her.

"Oh, no!" I said.

Jimmy chuckled out loud without even looking at

me. "She's all runned over," he said. Back and forth went the fire engine over the Playskool nurse, who was lying on her side with her head turned around 180 degrees.

"Now she's going for a walk!" the monster-child said, grabbing the Playskool nurse again. "Walk, walk, walk," he said as he bumped her along one side of the couch and up onto the back. "Walk, walk, walk," he said, starting to smile, and he turned and looked at me. Halfway across the back of the sofa, he let go, and the Playskool nurse fell down behind the couch.

"Oh, no!" I said again.

"She fell off!" Jimmy cried delightedly. "The mommy's dead." He crawled back behind the couch, picked up the Playskool doll, and dropped her all over again. "Bad, *bad* mommy!" he yelled.

Somehow Jimmy Benton's little game seemed familiar to me, and all of a sudden I knew.

I don't remember much at all about Mama dying. I think I remember the funeral. At least I remember a room full of flowers and Aunt Sally picking me up and crying. But Dad says that for a long time after Mama died, I talked about my bad, bad mama. I don't remember that part at all.

"Why did I say *that*?" I asked when he told me.

"Because you were angry that she left you."

"But she *died*!"

"I know," Dad said.

"She couldn't help it!" I told him.

"But *you* didn't know that," Dad said. "You probably thought that if she'd really wanted to stay alive and take care of you, she would have."

I remember thinking about that for a long time. "How did I get over it?" I asked finally.

And Dad had said, "We just let you get your anger out, Al, that's all."

I knew then what I could do to help Jimmy Benton.

"Boy, Jimmy is *really* mad!" I said.

He just laughed. Up went the Playskool nurse over the back of the couch again. Clunk. Down she fell on the other side.

"There she goes again!" I said.

For the next hour, the Playskool nurse was run over by the fire engine again, stuck feet first in a cement mixer, dropped from an airplane, dumped out of a car, and finally deposited upside down in a jar of paste.

"That fixes her good!" I said.

Jimmy screeched with laughter.

All that violence must have tired him out, because he settled down at last for a story. He wanted more grape juice, too, and this time he drank it all.

At five o'clock, we played a game to see which one of us would see his mother's car first. When I saw the Bentons' station wagon turn the corner, I pretended to look the other way.

"She's here!" Jimmy yelled, and was waiting at the door when she came in. He didn't hug back when she hugged him, but at least he didn't hit her.

"How was he?" she asked.

"We had a fine time," I said. I didn't tell her that during the course of the afternoon she had been chopped, dropped, and run over.

I thought a lot about Jimmy as I walked back down the block. Dad says it took me a long time to get over Mama's death. Sometimes I think I'm not over it yet. Over the anger part, maybe, but not over the wanting and missing.

6
The Up-Lift Spandex Ahh-Bra

THE NEXT DAY, something really weird happened to Pamela. She'd never had any more bosom than I did, and even though she wore those T-shirts with the deep V in front, there was hardly anything down there to see. But that day, when we all met at the playground after supper as usual, Pamela was definitely larger. Not just lumps under the T-shirt, but the skin showing in the V-neck looked puffed out. I couldn't stop staring.

Patrick, Mark, and Tom were there, so even though both Elizabeth and I noticed the way Pamela's chest was swelling, we couldn't ask her about it until the boys went out into the field to throw Mark's football around. Then we both asked it together:

"Pamela, what happened?"

She pretended she didn't know what we were talking about, of course, as though anybody could get a sudden swelling of the breasts overnight.

"What?" she said, pushing her feet hard on the ground and leaning back as the swing came forward.

"Your breasts!" I said.

"Oh, those," said Pamela. "It's a new kind of bra."

I didn't know how any bra could puff your *skin* up. But there was Pamela, big as life.

"What *kind* of bra?" asked Elizabeth. We both wanted to rush right out and buy one.

"The Up-Lift Spandex Ahh-Bra," Pamela said, as though she had invented it herself.

"How does it *do* that?" I asked.

"Come over tomorrow afternoon and I'll show it to you," she said.

"I've got to baby-sit Jimmy Benton," I said.

"I've got a ballet lesson," said Elizabeth.

"Then I'll bring one over here tomorrow night and you can see it," Pamela promised.

I spent all the next day waiting for the evening, and when the evening was over, I wished it had never happened.

There's something about boys I can't explain. I don't think girls would ever do what Mark Stedmeister did that night. Even Patrick got crazy. Most of the time he was polite. I mean, he opened doors for me and always walked on the outside of the sidewalk, which I never saw any other boy do in my life. I asked him once why he did it, and he said his dad taught him.

"But *why*?" I asked.

"So if a car splashes water at us, I'll get it instead of you," he told me. It's sort of nice, I guess, when you think about it.

Anyway, Patrick was polite most of the time, but he wasn't on this particular evening, and neither was Tom Perona. The boys were fooling around on the monkey bars, chinning themselves to impress us and trying to see who could get up highest and stay there longest. Pamela, Elizabeth, and I were sitting on a bench near the swings.

"I brought one," Pamela whispered. "I haven't even worn it yet. Mom bought me two."

She pulled a little sack out of her shoulder bag—Pamela is the only one of us who carries a purse wherever she goes because she always carries a brush and makeup—and we leaned over to see.

"The Up-Lift Spandex Ahh-Bra," read the tag attached to one strap.

"Here's the secret," Pamela explained. "There's a little nylon pad in the bottom of each bra cup, and that pushes your breast up so that it puffs out over the top."

It was the most amazing thing I had ever seen.

"A gentle assist to the undersized," it read on the back of the tag. "Lifts, supports, and promotes cleavage."

"What's cleavage?" Elizabeth asked, taking the sack from Pamela and examining the nylon pads.

"Where the breasts come together," I said knowingly. "When you have a lot of cleavage you can wear a gold locket and it almost gets buried between your breasts." I dreamed of having enough cleavage some day to be able to bury a locket in it.

I was just about to ask Pamela where her mother bought the bra when all of a sudden we realized that the boys were awfully quiet, and just as we looked up to see that they weren't on the monkey bars anymore, Mark Stedmeister reached around from behind us, grabbed the bra out of Elizabeth's hands, and went running as fast as he could go across the playground, holding the bra up in the air like a flag and shrieking like a savage.

Pamela screamed, and Elizabeth and I stared in horror as he circled the basketball court three times and then climbed to the top of the monkey bars and sat down. Pamela put her hands over her face.

"Mark!" I yelled. "Give that back!"

Patrick and Tom were laughing. The thing was, when Mark Stedmeister grabbed the bra out of Elizabeth's hands, he thought it was hers.

"Presenting . . ." he said, and made a noise like a trumpet, "the . . ." and he found the tag and read it aloud, ". . . the Up-Lift Spandex Ahh-Bra! Ta da!"

Pamela was crying. I could tell by the way her shoulders shook. Now Patrick and Tom were crawling up the bars to see the bra.

"Mark, you are absolutely awful!" Elizabeth called up at him.

Mark went on reading the tag: "A gentle assist

to the undersized. Lifts, supports, and promotes cleavage!"

Pamela slid off the bench and sat there on the grass with her head on her knees. Mark didn't even notice. He slipped his arms through the straps of the bra and pretended he was wearing it. Patrick and Tom doubled over with laughter.

"I dreamed I was climbing the jungle gym in my Maidenform bra," yelled Mark, and this time Patrick almost fell off the monkey bars he was laughing so hard. He was positively disgusting. "Hey, Elizabeth, if you want your bra back, come and get it!" Mark yelled, and acted as though he were going to tie it to the top of the jungle gym.

Elizabeth glowered at him. "That's not mine," she said icily.

Mark looked at me.

"It's not mine either," I said.

Mark Stedmeister suddenly stopped grinning and stared down at Pamela, who was just a little heap now on the grass.

"Well, heck!" he said. "I thought it was Elizabeth's." As though that excused him. "Hey, Elizabeth," he said. "Catch." And he threw the bra at her as though it had suddenly turned into a hot potato.

Elizabeth caught it and stuffed it back in the sack. We crouched down beside Pamela on the ground.

"I got it back, Pamela," Elizabeth told her.

"I want to die," said Pamela.

I couldn't help but be a little bit glad that she was

finding out how I felt when she sent that love note to Patrick and signed my name, but even I knew that this was worse. A *lot* worse.

Slowly Pamela got to her feet. Mark Stedmeister stayed at the top of the jungle gym, and I knew he wasn't about to come down for anything.

"I never want to see Mark Stedmeister again as long as I live," said Pamela.

What was she *saying*? She couldn't break up with him now. Seventh grade was only a little over a month off, and then where would she be?

We started walking Pamela home, Elizabeth on one side of her, me on the other. Was this the first breakup we were going to have in our group? None of us had been through it before, and we didn't quite know how to act. So we just walked off the playground without saying good-bye to anyone, not even Tom and Patrick.

"Now everyone knows," Pamela wept when we got out to the sidewalk.

"Knows what?" I asked.

"That I'm undersized!" Pamela wailed.

"Everybody knew that before," Elizabeth said, trying to be helpful. It was not helpful. Pamela cried all the harder.

"I don't think Mark really minds about your breast size," I said.

"I don't *care* what Mark thinks! Mark is a creep!" Pamela said, and the tears came even faster. I think we thought that all boys were creeps that night.

When we sat on Pamela's front steps and listened to her talk about getting even, though, I wondered how you could really like a boy one day and talk about making him miserable the next.

"If you ever see Mark Stedmeister with spinach between his teeth, don't tell him," she said. We promised.

"If you ever see him with his zipper open, don't say a word."

We promised that, too. Nothing was too awful for Mark Stedmeister.

"Don't ever speak to him again unless he apologizes," Pamela added. I didn't promise that one right away because "ever" is a long time. But when I thought about how awful Pamela had felt when he read the label on her bra, I knew I had to stick by her, so I promised.

We sat on Pamela's steps for about fifteen minutes before we saw the boys coming down the street.

"Here they come," said Elizabeth disgustedly.

"Wait till they get even with the house next door and then we'll get up and go inside," said Pamela. "We want to make sure they know we saw them."

It was like a movie on television. As soon as the boys got even with the house next door, we got up and went inside, and Pamela slammed the door hard. Then we ran upstairs to her bedroom and sat at the window in the darkness, watching.

We thought they'd come up on the porch and

ring the bell, but they didn't. They stood out under the street light and called to us.

"Hey, Pamela!" Mark bellowed.

"Elizabeth!" called Tom.

"Al-ice!" yelled Patrick.

It was like a zoo. The yelling went on for about five minutes. We didn't get up and go down, and they didn't come any closer.

Pamela's mother tapped on the bedroom door. "Is this going to go on all night?" she asked.

"We're not speaking," Pamela explained.

"Well, then go out there and tell them," Mrs. Jones said and went back downstairs. Obviously, she didn't understand.

"Why don't we go on home and maybe they'll stop yelling," I suggested to Elizabeth. We stood up and groped our way across Pamela's bedroom toward the door.

"Wait," said Pamela, grabbing for our arms. "Don't you speak to Tom or Patrick either until Mark apologizes to me."

"Hey!" I said. "What did Patrick do?"

"He laughed," said Pamela. "So did Tom."

"But how will they know what's wrong unless we tell them?" I asked.

Pamela thought about it. I could just see the outline of her face there in the darkness, the silhouette of her long yellow hair. "Well, you can tell him that none of us is going to speak to any of them until Mark Stedmeister apologizes to me," said Pamela.

This was getting more and more complicated by the minute.

"Promise!" Pamela demanded.

"Elizabeth and Tom aren't even going together yet," I said, trying to stall.

"I promise anyway," said Elizabeth. "We have to stick together or no telling what they'll do next. That was just too awful for words." They both turned toward me.

"I can't promise that," I said uncomfortably. "It doesn't seem fair to Patrick, even though he was a jerk for laughing."

"Alice, think what Mark did to me!" Pamela said indignantly. "He humiliated me, and Patrick thought it was funny!"

"Well, it *was,* Pamela, in a way," I said. Oh, boy, was *that* ever the wrong thing to say.

"Alice McKinley, you're not my friend either!" Pamela said. "And I don't think I'll even speak to you until *you* apologize!"

"Oh, Pamela, come on!" I said, but she ran down the hall to the bathroom and locked herself in.

I didn't know what to do. Elizabeth and I left, walking as fast as we could so we wouldn't have to speak to the boys. They called after us and followed us for about half a block, staying some distance behind, and then they stopped. I was hoping that Patrick would follow me home so I could explain it to him, but he didn't.

Elizabeth went on over to her house and I went

inside mine. I waited for Patrick to at least call me on the phone. He didn't do that either.

It's weird. When Patrick and I first started going together in sixth grade, everything seemed so simple. We just walked to school together and ate lunch at the same table and that was that.

But now we were all mixed up with Pamela and Elizabeth, who weren't speaking to Mark and Tom, and I decided that I didn't care what kind of support and cleavage the Up-Lift Spandex Ahh-Bra could give. I didn't want one for anything in the world.

7
The Music Lesson

WHEN I WAS in Chicago over spring vacation and we were talking about boys, Aunt Sally happened to mention that a girl should never call a boy on the telephone. "It just isn't done," she said.

There were so many rules to having a boyfriend that I wondered why somebody didn't put out a manual. When Dad bought a new car, he got an owner's manual. I don't know why a boy and girl can't get one when they start going together for the first time. Girls don't phone boys, boys walk on the outside of the sidewalk, you can't give any presents that touch the skin. . . . Dad even told me that when you're going upstairs, the girl goes first but when you're going downstairs, the boy goes first. How do you ever know these things? Who decides?

"It's just common sense," Dad explained. "The man is always supposed to be in a position to assist a lady if necessary. He walks behind her on the stairs so that if she falls backward he can catch her. He walks ahead of her going downstairs in case she falls forward."

I tried to figure out how that would help. I imagined Patrick walking ahead of me down a long flight of stairs, me tripping and falling forward, bumping into Patrick, and both of us tumbling down together. I tried to see the etiquette in that.

The big problem right then, however, was not knowing how to fall down the stairs gracefully but whether or not to phone Patrick. There we were the night before, all set to have a good time on the swings, when suddenly Pamela wasn't speaking to Mark and Elizabeth wasn't speaking to Tom and I wasn't supposed to say anything to Patrick. Somebody had to explain something to someone. Elizabeth would *never* have a steady boyfriend by seventh grade at this rate.

It took me half the night to decide to call him the next day, and then it took two hours to get up my nerve.

First of all, his mom would probably answer. Patrick doesn't have any brothers or sisters, and his dad would be at work. I had never met his mother. I knew that when you called someone, you were supposed to say who you were. Should I just say my first name if his mother answered, or should I say, "This is Alice

McKinley"? If I just said, "Alice," it would sound as though she already knew me, as though I assumed that Patrick talked about me all the time. And was I supposed to say a few polite things to her first if she answered, or ask for Patrick right away?

I rehearsed all the different ways to talk to Patrick's mother, and the longer I rehearsed, the drier my mouth got and the sweatier my hands became. In desperation, I just grabbed the phone, dialed, and said, when his mom answered, "Is Patrick there?"

"Just a minute," said the voice at the other end. It was the kind of voice where you can't tell anything at all from it. Was she nice? Was she bossy? I heard Patrick pick up the phone.

"Yeah?"

"This is Alice," I said.

"Hi," said Patrick.

I waited to see if he'd talk first—give me a clue about what he was thinking. He didn't.

"I wanted to explain about last night," I said, and swallowed. "I've probably lost Pamela as a friend because I'm not supposed to talk to you ever again unless Mark Stedmeister apologizes to her."

"Well, that's the dumbest thing I ever heard. What's that got to do with me?" Patrick asked incredulously.

"You laughed," I said miserably.

"Laughed?"

"At Pamela's bra."

"I was laughing at Mark *wearing* the bra. It could have been *anybody's* bra, I still would have laughed," said Patrick.

He didn't sound very sorry to me. How did boys go from being such jerks to people that grown-up women wanted to marry?

"Well, Pamela's awfully hurt," I said coldly.

"Pamela would be hurt if you hit her with a marshmallow," said Patrick.

Was this going to be our first quarrel? Was it going to start out with Pamela's bra and end up with my not having a boyfriend to open my locker for me in seventh grade?

"Anyway, things are all patched up now," Patrick told me.

"What?"

"They made up—Mark and Pamela."

"They *did*?"

"Yeah. Mark went back later and took her some Whitman's chocolates."

"What?"

"And he's taking her roller skating tonight."

"He *is*?"

Suddenly I was furious. Here I had worried half the night and most of this morning about how I could explain things to Patrick, and all the while Pamela was at home eating Whitman's chocolates and getting ready to go roller skating. I could have killed her.

"Want me to come over?" Patrick asked.

"Yes," I said. "I do."

I called Pamela. "What's the big idea?" I demanded.

"Alice, I would have told you, honestly, but I've been so busy washing and drying my hair I just haven't had time!"

I suppose when you have hair so long you can sit on it, it *does* take a long time to do it, but I figured Pamela could have found a minute somewhere to call. I began to suspect that she wanted to eat all the best chocolates herself so that by the time she got around to telling Elizabeth and me that she and Mark had made up over a Whitman's Sampler, there would only be coconut and jelly centers left.

I put on my tapered jeans and a thin gauze shirt and was waiting out on the porch when Patrick arrived. I leaned against a post, my face turned up toward the sun, my curls tumbling—well, sort of— around my shoulders, and I smiled at him like all those women in the shampoo ads.

"What's the matter? Crick in your neck?" Patrick asked, as he got off his bike and came up the steps.

I stopped smiling my shampoo-girl smile and sat down on the swing.

I was glad that we had talked about last night before it had turned into a real quarrel. Now all we had to do was get through the last five weeks of summer and maybe we'd still be going together when we started junior high. Patrick put one hand over mine in the swing and we pushed our feet against the floor. The swing began to move, and everything was back to normal.

And then it happened.

I think Patrick was still thinking about the night before. "Do you know the song, 'Sorry Doesn't Make It Right'?" he asked.

I nodded. It was one of my favorite songs, probably because I heard it so much. Lester played it all the time. It's about how it isn't enough just to say you're sorry when you hurt someone, you've got to really change.

"I was thinking about that on the way over here," he said, "but I can't remember a certain part." He started to sing it then, slowing the swing down a little to keep in time:

" 'Sorry's sugar from your lips, a cotton candy cane. . . .' What's the rest of it?"

" 'Words can help, but just so much, you've got to really change,' " I told him.

"Yeah, that's it, but how does the melody go?"

My stomach turned over. "I . . . I don't know," I said.

"I thought you said you knew it."

"Well . . . Lester plays it all the time."

"Then *think*, Alice. Just hum it with me and see if it comes to you." He started humming the part again about "Sorry's sugar from your lips . . ." I didn't make a sound.

"*You* hum it," he said.

My stomach seemed to be moving up into my chest. My throat.

"I . . . I can't," I said in a half whisper.

"Why not?" Patrick was staring at me now.

"I can't sing," I said simply.

It was as though I'd said I couldn't breathe or something.

"Not at all?" he asked.

I shook my head.

"What happened?"

"What do you mean, what happened? I've never been able to carry a tune. I'm tone deaf."

"But . . ." Patrick kept on staring. This was as bad as Mark Stedmeister with Pamela's bra. This was *worse.* "But your dad plays the violin! Lester plays the guitar! Your father runs a music store!"

"So I'm the family moron," I said sullenly.

"Hey, Alice, I didn't mean that. I just think you're too hard on yourself. I don't think you've given yourself a chance."

"Patrick," I said, "in grade school, when our class sang for the PTA meetings, I played the triangle instead. You don't know what you're talking about."

"I'll bet you just got embarrassed once and never got over it, that's all," he said.

"I tried singing at every birthday party up until I was eight and they almost sent me home," I said, exaggerating.

"Come on," said Patrick, and without waiting for an answer, he went inside the house and sat down at

Dad's piano. I could feel little trickles of sweat running down my back.

"Patrick," I said, "I am not going to make a fool of myself in front of you."

This time Patrick looked me straight in the eye. "Alice, there's no way you can make a fool of yourself in front of me. I like you too much for that."

Something warm and mushy filled my chest when he said that, and I believed him. Sometimes Patrick talks like a twenty-year-old man. I knew that while he may have laughed at Mark Stedmeister wearing Pamela's bra, he wasn't going to laugh at me no matter how bad I sounded.

He played a note on the piano. "Listen," he said, and played it again. "Now see if you can hum it."

I hummed.

Patrick looked at me sort of strangely. "Listen again," he said, and pressed down the same key.

I hummed again.

"Does that sound right to you?" he asked curiously.

"What do you mean 'right'? I hummed, didn't I?"

"But it wasn't the same note."

"That's what I've been trying to tell you."

"You can't tell the difference?"

"What difference?"

"You can't tell they're not the same? Listen. I'll play the note and you hum at the same time."

Patrick played the note. I hummed. It sounded like a two-toned horn.

"I guess it's not the same," I said.

Patrick looked jubilant. "See? See? You *can* tell the difference. All you need is practice, Alice."

I couldn't believe I'd done something right.

"You were singing too low," Patrick explained. "You've got to come up a couple of notes."

Low? Up?

"Patrick," I said. "I haven't the slightest idea what you are talking about."

"Listen." Patrick played a bunch of notes on the piano, one after another. "Each note is getting higher, right?"

"I guess so," I said.

"Listen again," said Patrick. He played another bunch of notes. "These are getting lower."

I could hear that each one sounded different from the note before, but that was about all I knew.

"Now," said Patrick at last, and played a note on the piano again. "See if you can hum it this time. Try to hear it in your head before you start." He played the note.

I tried. I could feel sweat under my arms.

"Can't you come up a little higher, Alice?"

I stood on my tiptoes and hummed again.

Patrick stared at me in disbelief. "That's *lower*!"

I shrugged. "So there you have it, Patrick."

"*Try,* Alice! Once more." He played the note. I hummed.

"Almost!" he said. "Just a little higher."

This time I must have done it.

"Good!" Patrick yelled. He played another note. "Now try this." I hummed again.

"No, that's the same one you hummed before. Now you have to go lower."

I tried.

"*Lower,* Alice! Not higher!"

I could feel angry tears in my eyes. I gave a loud hum. An *angry* hum. This time even *I* could tell that it was so far off it was ridiculous.

And suddenly I went back out on the porch, plunked myself down on the swing, and swallowed and swallowed, trying to keep from crying.

Patrick came out and sat down beside me. He knew I was crying but he had the decency not to stare at me then. He put one hand over mine.

"I'm sorry," he said. "I won't do that again."

That night I was helping Dad make lasagna for dinner and told him about the music lesson that never got off the ground.

"I've always wondered about you, Al," Dad said. "Just seems so unusual, really, in a whole family full of singers."

I flared up at Dad. "So have me tested! Send me to a special school! Operate!"

"Listen, Al, you have so many good things going for you, I can't even count them all," Dad said. "As far as I'm concerned, you don't have to sing again in your life unless you want to, and I won't say another word about it."

I smiled a little.

"Do you like me?" I asked, playing our little game.

"Rivers," said Dad.

"Love me?"

"Oceans," he said, and gave me a hug, right there over the mozzarella.

He left me alone in the kitchen to make the salad, and while I worked I sang that song to myself:

> "Sorry's sugar from your lips,
> A cotton candy cane,
> Words can help, but just so much,
> You've got to really change."

I didn't know about the music, but I got the words right, and to me, I sounded just fine.

8
Couples

ELIZABETH CALLED me at eleven o'clock two nights later, just after I'd crawled into bed. She sounded breathless and far away.

"Speak louder, Elizabeth," I said, after I'd answered the phone in the upstairs hall.

"I can't," she told me.

"Where are you?"

"In the closet."

"The closet?"

"I don't want Mom and Dad to hear."

"What's *wrong*?" I asked.

"Nothing! It's wonderful! Come over quick and I'll tell you."

I ran across the street barefoot and sat on her steps in my pajamas.

"In this very exact spot," said Elizabeth, sitting

down beside me, "only twenty minutes ago, Tom asked me to go with him."

I gave a squeal, then stopped. "Why can't you tell your mother?"

"She'd be furious!" Elizabeth said. "I'm not supposed to go with a boy till I get to high school."

I kept wondering who makes the rules. Pamela's not supposed to kiss till she's sixteen, Elizabeth's not supposed to go steady until high school. . . . I just don't understand how one day you aren't ready for something and then, after a birthday party, you are.

"Tell me everything," I said eagerly.

"Well . . ." Elizabeth got breathless again. "We were holding hands and he was sort of looking the other way and swallowing and then he looked back and said, 'Elizabeth, will you go with me?' "

"And then what?"

"I said yes, and he squeezed my hand and took off his ID bracelet and put it on my wrist." She held out her arm so I could see.

"He put it on for you? He fastened it and everything?" I ran one finger over the shiny metal bracelet. Oh, wow. This was about the most romantic thing I'd ever heard.

"Yes." Elizabeth hugged her knees and sort of moaned.

"Then what?"

"Then I told him to wait here, and I went upstairs and got one of my school pictures and gave it to him, and he put it in his wallet."

I moaned, too. All of us—Elizabeth, Pamela, and I—had been doing a lot of moaning lately, but it was just too wonderful for words. Patrick and I had been going with each other longer than anyone else so far, and we still hadn't exchanged pictures or bracelets or anything.

"What if your mother sees the bracelet?" I asked suddenly.

"She won't. I'll never wear it in the house. I have a special place for it in a velvet box in my drawer," Elizabeth said. "We're three couples now. Isn't that wonderful, Alice? We'll all have boyfriends when we start seventh grade."

The next night we started walking round the neighborhood holding hands, the six of us—the couples, I mean. Up until then we'd just been horsing around the playground, but now that we were all officially couples, we'd just walk in the summer darkness and sometimes we'd kiss in the shadows. We'd kid around under the streetlights, too, and the boys would get silly, and sometimes we'd go to High's for ice cream, but we spent most of the time just walking. Elizabeth and Tom never held hands until we were at least a block away from the Prices' house.

Each couple had a style. Pamela and Mark Stedmeister always walked in front, with their arms around each other and, if they were wearing jeans, with their hands in each other's back pocket. I don't think I could ever do that—put my hand in Patrick's pocket. Right over his hip, I mean. I can imagine what Aunt Sally would say about that.

Elizabeth and Tom usually walked in the middle and they just held hands. They never kissed in the dark places, either. They were very polite. If their hips happened to bump into each other, Elizabeth always said, "Excuse me," and Tom kept in step with Elizabeth.

For some reason, Patrick and I always walked at the end. I guess we just felt more comfortable, not being on display for the others to watch. Sometimes we kissed and sometimes we held hands, but a lot of the time we'd catch lightning bugs and put them on each other's shoulders, or pick leaves off trees as we passed, or just talk.

When we got to High's, we'd all order ice cream in cups so we'd have an excuse to hang around the store to eat it and drop the cups in the trash can before we left. You never knew who you'd see at High's, and it was sort of nice to be one of the couples and have kids from school walk in and see you. We'd order one of their exotic flavors—Heavenly Hash or Rum Pecan—and then we'd stand there making up flavors of our own: Chocolate Syrup Fudge Brownie Chip or Strawberry Marshmallow Banana Mint. We even gave our suggestions to the manager once, and he said, "Look, all I do is work here." One night Mark was showing us how he could fake a burp and the manager asked us to leave. The next night when we were eating ice cream, though, Elizabeth belched accidentally, and the manager even frowned at her.

I don't know if this was what started it or not, but we'd been going to High's for about a week when Elizabeth began getting weird about food. Every night when we'd get in High's she'd say she wasn't hungry, and when Tom would order something for her anyway, she'd get red in the face and hardly even touch it. So one day when Pamela and I were at her house in the afternoon, we came right out and asked: "Elizabeth, what's wrong?"

At first she acted as though she didn't know what we were talking about, but finally she said she was just too embarrassed about eating to do it in public.

"It's disgusting," she said. "Think about it. You put food in your mouth and it gets all mixed up with spit and you chew it up into a revolting mess and swallow it. And we're supposed to do all that in front of boys?"

"Elizabeth, it's only ice cream!" Pamela told her. "They do it in front of us!"

"But it *could* be something else," said Elizabeth. "Have you ever looked at food after you've chewed it awhile?"

"You've been chewing ever since you had teeth," I said. "What's happened all of a sudden?"

"I don't know," Elizabeth said miserably. "The longer I go without eating in front of Tom, the scarier it gets."

Pamela and I told Elizabeth that if she didn't start

eating soon when Tom was around, the boys would start staring at her and that would make it all the worse. And we told her that if she would eat her ice cream the next time we went to High's, we'd distract the boys so that no one would be watching her.

The following night at High's, Elizabeth ordered a small dish of French vanilla, and Pamela and I started balancing our plastic spoons on our noses. It was a good thing it was the manager's night off, because he would have sent Pamela and me out of the store, but pretty soon we had the boys doing it, too, and the next time we looked, Elizabeth had finished her French vanilla.

"Thanks, Alice," she told me later.

The next night, though, just as we were leaving, Tom bought a package of potato chips and we stood out under the streetlight eating them. Even Elizabeth took one. I don't know how it happened, but the exact second Elizabeth popped it in her mouth was the exact second everybody stopped talking, and a loud crackling, popping sound came from Elizabeth's mouth. She was mortified.

"Wow! What's that? Your teeth?" Mark Stedmeister said, and the next day Pamela and I had to distract the boys again in order to get Elizabeth to eat a potato chip.

We were talking about it on Saturday when Pamela and Elizabeth came over to sun in my backyard. We stretched out on the grass in our bathing suits.

"It's *bodies*!" Elizabeth told us. "I mean, they're so embarrassing."

"Everybody's got one," I said.

"The *noises* they make!" she said. "I have to eat four crackers just before I go out with Tom to keep my stomach from growling."

Now that's the kind of thing you learn from a mother. I never in my life knew that the way to stop your stomach from growling was to eat four crackers before you went somewhere. When it happened in class, I usually just folded my arms across my abdomen or pressed my history book against my stomach.

Pamela lifted one leg up in the air and smeared some more suntan lotion on her thigh. "The thing about bodies that bothers me is how women can stand to have babies," she said.

"I can't even think about it," said Elizabeth. "When my mind even *starts* to think about it, I switch to something else."

"Do you suppose it hurts a lot?" Pamela asked, looking at me.

"Why are you asking *me*?" I bleated. "I don't even have a mother!"

"It can't be too terrible or women would just have one baby and stop," Pamela said.

"Let's don't talk about it," said Elizabeth.

Pamela flopped over on her stomach and grinned. "Now, *making* babies might be nice."

"Don't *talk* about it!" Elizabeth warned, so Pamela shut up.

Sometimes I don't understand Elizabeth at all. If I had a mother, I'll bet we'd talk about things like that all the time. I asked Dad once if having a baby hurt much, and he said that Mama sometimes said she'd rather have a baby than go to the dentist. That didn't make me feel much better about dentists.

"What bothers me most," said Elizabeth, "is how you can tell a boy that you have to go to the bathroom. Even if you say *rest room,* he'll know."

"Everybody goes to the bathroom, Elizabeth," I said.

"But they don't have to *know* that you do," she said.

I stared at her. "Elizabeth, if people thought you *didn't* go to the bathroom, they'd really think you were strange."

"But it's so gross! I've decided that if I'm ever out with a boy and I have to use the rest room, I'll just tell him I want to wash my hands."

I told Dad and Lester about that at dinner.

"Well," Dad said, "some people love to make up things to worry about."

I looked at Lester. "What does Crystal Harkins say when you're out on a date and she has to use the rest room?"

"Crystal just says, 'I have to go,' " Lester told me. He was staring at me strangely. "Al," he said, "what happened to you?"

I got up and looked in the mirror. When we were lying out in the sun that afternoon, I'd kept a towel folded up over my eyes. My forehead was red, my cheeks and nose and chin were red, but the strip across my eyes was as white as a boiled egg. I shrieked.

The next day I was lying out on the grass with Elizabeth, getting a suntan, and I had everything covered up except my eyes. I told Elizabeth about Crystal Harkins—how she was pretty and had a big bosom and played the clarinet, and how I'd seen her in a concert once in a black velvet dress, and she'd looked like the Queen of Sheba or something. And I said that when Crystal Harkins was out with my brother and needed to use the bathroom, she just said, "I have to go," just like that.

I don't know if it helped Elizabeth or not. But by the middle of August, she was eating ice cream regularly in front of Tom, she wasn't saying "Excuse me" anymore when they accidentally bumped hips, and she finally got to the point where she even ate a potato chip on the street corner. Politely. With her lips closed.

9
What Happened at Jimmy's

THE SCARY PART about having a boyfriend, I guess, is that you're never sure what will happen next. In some ways, that's the nice part. You always wonder. With me, though, I worried more than I wondered. The closer you get to someone, the closer you want to be. How close is too close? How close isn't close enough?

Pamela said that when boys get together to talk, they use a secret language.

"What?" I said.

"They pretend they're talking baseball, but they're really talking about how far they went with a girl."

"What?" I said again. This was the most unbelievable thing I had ever heard.

"It's true!" Pamela said. "If they talk about getting to first base, it means they held hands with their girl. If they talk about getting to second base, it means they got as far as a kiss. If they say they got to third base, it means they put one hand up under her T-shirt, and if they say they made it all the way to home, it means . . ."

"I don't want to *hear* about it!" Elizabeth said, putting her hands over her ears. If Elizabeth ever found herself alone in a house with a boy, I don't know what she would do.

But that's what happened to me. One Thursday it was raining and Patrick couldn't mow lawns so he called me at the Bentons' and asked if he could come over for a while. Something told me that this wasn't quite right when you were on a job, but Mrs. Benton hadn't said I couldn't, and I knew that Pamela let Mark come over all the time when she was baby-sitting, so I said yes.

Jimmy Benton and I were getting along pretty well. His favorite game still was to run over the Playskool nurse with his fire truck, but because I let him and didn't scold, this happened less, and during the third week, when he was eating his graham cracker, he even gave the Playskool nurse a bite. We were making progress.

Some days were better than others, of course. When he missed his mother the most, Jimmy would crawl around the floor pretending he was a dog and would try to bite my knees, but I'd get him to do tricks instead: "Roll over"; "Sit up"; "Play dead" (especially "Play dead").

That day when Patrick came over, Jimmy had a fine time, and Patrick was really good with him. Patrick would build things out of Jimmy's blocks and let him run over them with his cement mixer, or he would crawl around on the floor with Jimmy on his back. It was sort of as if we were playing house— Daddy, Mommy, and little Jimmy Benton.

When Jimmy took his nap, Patrick and I had the house to ourselves, and this was really embarrassing. At home, Patrick and I sat out on the porch, but here we were, with the Bentons away, and there I was on the couch, with Patrick's arm around me.

I could tell by the way Patrick was looking at me that things were going to go a little further here than they had back home on my front porch, and I was nervous. He pulled me closer to him than he usually did. I closed my eyes when he leaned over to kiss me, but this time, I could feel his tongue pushing against my lips, pushing them open, and then he ran his tongue along my teeth. A French kiss!

I felt my palms begin to sweat. I hadn't brushed my teeth after lunch! There could be all kinds of crud on my teeth! I tried to remember what I'd had for lunch. Pizza! A piece of Lester's leftover pizza, and I'll bet it was just loaded with garlic.

The kiss went on so long I wondered when I was allowed to swallow. What were the rules about this? Should the boy let you up for air every ten seconds or were you supposed to sort of keep your nostrils to one side?

And then Patrick's tongue was pushing against my teeth. I couldn't let him touch my tongue! Couldn't let him taste the garlic pizza!

Suddenly I backed away.

"Patrick," I said. "I . . . I don't think I'm ready for this yet."

"Okay," said Patrick. He looked a little relieved himself.

I was glad when Jimmy woke up early and we all went out in the kitchen for a snack. I poured some apple juice for Jimmy and gave him a graham cracker. We found some grapes in the refrigerator, too, and Patrick put five of them on Jimmy's tray while we ate the others.

Patrick was in a silly mood. He sat down in a chair, tipped his head way back, and tried to see how high he could throw a grape and still catch it in his mouth when it fell. Whenever he missed, Jimmy screeched with delight. I began to think that Patrick was a better baby-sitter than I was. Finally I climbed up on a chair and held a grape up as high as I could, then dropped it. This time Patrick caught it and made a big "Whomp" sound. Jimmy howled. I did it again, and again Patrick caught it. This time, though, we didn't hear anything from Jimmy, and when I turned to look, Jimmy's face was turning blue. I screamed.

Patrick leaped up.

"He's choking!" I cried, and felt my legs turn to rubber.

In an instant Patrick was around behind Jimmy's high chair, lifting Jimmy Benton up on his feet. "Hold him straight up!" he said to me.

My hands were shaking. I grabbed Jimmy's shoulders and held him up. Patrick slipped his arms around Jimmy's body, clasping his hands in front, just under Jimmy's ribs, and jerked his hands inward. Nothing happened. I was crying. Jimmy started to slump over.

"Hold him up straight!" Patrick yelled, and I grabbed Jimmy's shoulders firmly. This time Patrick brought his fist in harder against Jimmy's diaphragm, and *whoosh*—the grape shot out of Jimmy's mouth with a rush of air and hit the opposite wall.

Jimmy was crying, too, but he was breathing. I picked him up in my arms and took him in on the couch, holding him on my lap. Patrick came in and sat down at the other end of the couch. There was sweat on his forehead. We were both so scared we could hardly talk.

"H-He could have choked to death, Patrick," I said shakily. "If you weren't here, I wouldn't have known what to do."

"Yeah, but I wasn't sure I was doing it right. I think with little kids you have to be careful how you do it or you might break something."

"He would have choked!" I insisted.

"If I hadn't been here, we wouldn't have been goofing off," Patrick answered.

I knew that was true. Patrick also had no business giving grapes to Jimmy, and I had no business letting him. I couldn't believe I hadn't been more responsible.

"I think I'd better go," Patrick said. "You figure he's okay now?"

I checked Jimmy again. He was leaning against me, breathing quietly. I nodded. Patrick got up and went home. By the time Mrs. Benton came back, Jimmy and I were playing with clay on the kitchen table. I didn't say a word about Jimmy and the grape. The words just wouldn't come out.

At home that evening, I was in the kitchen with Dad and Lester cutting up celery for our stir-fry chicken, and I told them what had happened.

"That was pretty serious, Al," Dad said.

"I know."

"You ought to know the Heimlich maneuver," Lester said. "I thought they taught that in school. I learned it back in ninth grade."

"I'm only going into seventh," I reminded him.

"You choked on a piece of candy once when you were little, Al," Dad told me. "Your mother picked you up by your heels and shook you up and down."

"She did?"

"*I* remember that!" said Lester. "Mom whacked her on the back, too."

"Did it work?" I asked.

"You're here, aren't you?" Lester said. He

reached around and grabbed me, turned me upside down, and held me by my heels, bumping my head on the floor while I yelled bloody murder. The thing about Lester is, that's the way he shows he likes you.

After supper we went in the living room and had a lesson in the Heimlich maneuver. Lester demonstrated on Dad, Dad practiced on me, I practiced on Dad, and Lester gave us both an A plus.

"You'd better go to the library and read up on it, Al," Dad said. "See how it's done with small children. You've got to be prepared for things like that when you're a sitter."

I thought that would be the end of it, but when I went to the Bentons' again, Mrs. Benton said, "Jimmy said he got a grape stuck in his throat last Tuesday, Alice. Did that really happen or is it just one of his stories?"

I could have told Mrs. Benton that Jimmy just made it up, and I suppose she might have believed me, but I didn't want to start my first real job that way. I couldn't stand there in front of Jimmy Benton and say that what had happened wasn't true. My face got red and I swallowed a couple times, but finally I told Mrs. Benton the whole story. All except the French kissing part.

She was really nice about it, although I could tell by her face that she was frightened. She said she was partly to blame for not spelling out all the rules of the house, so we went over the ones she had missed:

1. No foods for Jimmy except what Mrs. Benton says he can have. Little kids can choke on all kinds of things, she told me.

2. No friends in the house.

3. Watching Jimmy the whole time he's awake, and every second he's eating.

I used to think that when I grew up there wouldn't be so many rules. Back in elementary school there were rules about what entrance you used in the mornings, what door you used going home, when you could talk in the library, how many paper towels you could use in the rest room, and how many drinks of water you could get during recess. And there was always somebody watching to make sure.

What I'm finding out about growing older is that there are just as many rules about lots of things, but there's nobody watching. Elizabeth, for example, isn't supposed to go with a boy till she's in high school, but her mother doesn't know. Pamela's not supposed to kiss until she's sixteen, but she does. Mrs. Benton doesn't really know for sure what goes on when I'm taking care of Jimmy; she just has to trust me. I wanted her to know that she could.

That night, I lay on top of my sheets, enjoying the breeze from the fan in my window, and thought some more about French kissing. I was really going to have to be careful what I ate from now on before I went out with Patrick. No more onions. No more cheese. No more garlic. How could I ever go to High's anymore and eat ice cream? How would I eat potato chips?

Patrick would be able to taste the salt on my teeth and tongue.

I curled up, my knees against my chest, and had a thought so scary that I hardly wanted to think about it. I felt like Elizabeth and the way she's always saying, "Don't *talk* about it! I won't *listen!*"

But this thought wouldn't go away. The more I tried not to think it, the more it was there: I wondered if maybe Patrick and I hadn't had more fun back in sixth grade when we were just eating lunch together, horsing around together at recess, and sitting out on my porch talking. Before the kissing began.

10
The Surf and Spray Hideaway

B Y THE LAST WEEK of August, I could see that the summer had had a certain rhythm to it. Patrick had called almost every morning and we'd decided what we were going to do that day, whether he was going to come over and play Monopoly on the porch or if we were just going to wait till after dinner and meet at the school with the others. On the days Patrick came over and I had work to do, he had always helped out. He scrubbed the front porch with me once: Patrick held the hose while I used the mop; every so often he'd spray me and I'd yell. He even helped Lester wash his car.

Sometimes the boys had gone bowling by themselves in the evening, or they'd ridden their bikes around the park, or somebody's father had driven them to Baltimore to see an Orioles game. Then it had just been Pamela and Elizabeth and me, and I'd liked those evenings, too. I hadn't had to worry about whether my shorts were too tight or my hair was too frizzy or if there was garlic on my breath. Sometimes we'd gotten up a girls' baseball team or all three of us had gone to a movie, and we'd had a fine time without the boys.

And by the end of August I'd begun to wonder if this was the way I was supposed to feel when Patrick wasn't there: relieved.

And then, that last week of August, I got a whole week of relief. Dad came home from work to say that Janice Sherman's beach house at Ocean City was empty, unexpectedly, and that Janice had offered it to us. I wasn't surprised because I think Janice is secretly in love with my father, and probably the only reason she didn't invite Dad to spend the week with her alone in the beach house is that she's assistant manager at the Melody Inn, and she can't take vacations at the same time Dad does.

Not only did Dad say we'd use her beach house, but he told me I could invite Pamela and Elizabeth to come, too. And just when I thought I wouldn't be able to go because I'd promised to baby-sit Jimmy Benton for the summer, Patrick volunteered to sit for me. And just when I thought Mrs. Benton would never agree to that, she said that if Patrick would come over and talk to her about it, she'd consider it. And just when I thought that *something* would happen to keep us from going, there we were—Pamela, Elizabeth, and I—in the back seat of Dad's Honda, heading for Ocean City.

All three of us said that we were going to miss our boyfriends while we were gone. All three of them said they were going to miss us. Elizabeth even brought Tom's ID bracelet along in her suitcase because she said it was important to wear it at the beach to show that she was "taken." And I let Patrick French-kiss me once before we left. I still couldn't decide whether I liked it or not, but it was certainly different.

Lester said he couldn't take off a week from work at Maytag, but that he would be down for the weekend, so it was just the four of us there in the Honda. Dad told me later that driving to Ocean City with three girls in the backseat was like listening to a Mozart flute concerto on a fast speed.

We went by Annapolis and then we stopped at the toll booth at the Bay Bridge where Pamela told the attendant he was a "hunk." Elizabeth and I dived down on the floor in embarrassment, and if Dad hadn't been driving he probably would have dived down, too. But then we were crossing the bridge and exclaiming over the sailboats below and begging Dad to turn up the volume on our favorite songs and asking Dad to stop at Stuckey's for a pecan fudge roll. We talked about all the teachers we had ever had and all the boys in the sixth grade who were good-looking, and when we saw a sign that said LOPES, 2 FOR $1.50, we asked Dad what they were, and he said melons. And when we saw a sign that said FEMALES, THREE DOLLARS A BUSHEL, we asked him what in the world *that* meant, and he said crabs. And finally, when we heard Dad say, "Thank the Good Lord in Heaven," we knew we were almost there.

It was a small beach house a block from the ocean with a wide front porch. Above the door was a piece of driftwood with the words "Surf and Spray Hideaway" painted on it. I wondered, when we walked inside, if Dad wasn't wishing he had come here with a sweetheart instead of three twelve-year-old girls. Sometimes I wonder about my dad. I don't think he's had any girlfriends at all since Mama died. He and Janice Sherman go to concerts sometimes, but I can tell by the way he comes right home afterward that he doesn't feel romantic toward her or anything.

Inside, there was a living room filled with wicker furniture and a kitchen in back, and three bedrooms and a bathroom upstairs. There was even a front porch *upstairs* with rocking chairs on it, just like the one below. One of the bedrooms had two sets of bunk beds, and Dad said that was where we were supposed to sleep.

The first thing we did was decide which bed each of us was going to sleep in. The second thing we did was dump all our stuff on our beds, and the third thing was put on our swimsuits and run down to the beach with our towels. The first thing Dad did was to put a Bach cassette on the stereo and go sit out on the porch. Now you can see why I worry about Dad.

We were in such a hurry to get to the beach that I didn't pay a lot of attention to what Pamela and Elizabeth were wearing till we got there. Elizabeth had on a blue and white suit with straps that crossed her back, and a little skirt in front. It looked something like a ballet costume, and on Elizabeth, it looked gorgeous.

Pamela had on a red and pink bikini and a little bra that had no straps.

"Pamela," I said, staring first at her navel and then at her bra. "How on earth are you going to keep that on in the water?"

"It's not for swimming, silly!" said Pamela.

"It's not?" I stared some more. "What's it for?"

"For the beach! For tanning!" Pamela told me.

"For boys to look at," Elizabeth said, and we laughed.

I felt really dumb-looking. I found out later that as soon as I invited Elizabeth and Pamela to go to the ocean with us, their mothers took them right out and bought them new bathing suits. I just threw in my same old yellow suit I'd worn the last two summers. It was one piece, made of a sort of stretchy material, and had a stain on the front where I'd dropped a chili dog. I could feel how tight it was across my thighs. The straps cut into my shoulders, and when I sat down on the sand, I felt as though it were going to cut me in half. I guess you could say it was too small. I think Aunt Sally sent it to me once, an old bathing suit of Carol's. I didn't even know how to buy a new one. I still wasn't sure how to buy a bra. I'd only learned the past year to buy my own Levis, for heaven's sake. Suddenly I wanted to be anywhere but on that beach between beautiful Elizabeth and gorgeous Pamela. Boys were looking at them already.

I decided to go back to the beach house and change into shorts. I'd wear shorts the whole week. I'd even go in the water wearing shorts if I had to.

"I'll be back," I told the girls, and made my way across the hot sand and down the block to the cottage.

Dad was still sitting on the porch.

"Back so soon?" he asked.

"Yeah," I said. "I think I'll put on shorts." I stopped and rinsed off my feet at the faucet by the steps.

"Where are the girls?" Dad asked.

"Down on the beach looking gorgeous," I said. I didn't really mean for it to sound so sour, but it did.

I started up the steps, but just as I reached the top, Dad said, "Al, isn't that the same bathing suit you were wearing last year?"

"And the year before that," I told him.

Dad put down his wineglass and stood up. "Put on your shorts," he said. "We're going shopping."

I just stared at him. Dad told me once he would rather go through a hurricane on crutches than go shopping, and here he was, suggesting it himself. I was back downstairs in three minutes flat, and five minutes later, we walked in the first shop we came to on the boardwalk.

"Yes, sir?" said a clerk, coming over.

"I want my daughter to have the most beautiful bathing suit you have, and I want it fitted properly," Dad told her.

I could hardly believe my ears. I didn't even know Dad knew how to *talk* to a salesclerk. He just smiled at me, and sat down on a chair to wait.

The clerk showed me a whole rack of suits my size. I picked six of them that I really liked, and when I tried them on, she showed me how they should fit, how they should feel, where there were wrinkles that shouldn't be.

A half hour later I left the shop wearing the most beautiful two-piece bathing suit I'd ever seen. It was sort of a shiny green and it had a bow in front between the breasts, and a bow on each side where the leg was cut high. I didn't even look like the same girl. I had gorgeous long legs and a nice bosom and I just hugged Dad when I came out and kept saying, "Thank you, thank you." I'll bet the salesclerk thought I was a little orphan girl he'd found under the boardwalk or something.

Dad took my other clothes on back to the cottage and I ran down to the water. Pamela and Elizabeth were lying on their backs with their eyes closed.

"No one was there," Pamela was saying. "I wonder where she went." She opened her eyes when she realized someone was standing there blocking the sun, and then she saw me.

"Alice?" she said, sitting up. "Where were you?"

Elizabeth opened her eyes and sat up, too.

"Alice!" Elizabeth said. "It's gorgeous! Where did you get it?"

"Dad just bought it for me," I said. "My other swimsuit was too small."

"Turn around," said Pamela.

I turned. Slowly. I saw some boys watching me. I blushed. Pamela whistled.

"I never saw someone change so much just because of a bathing suit!" Elizabeth said. I wasn't sure if that was a compliment or not, but I didn't care. It was one of the most wonderful afternoons of my life.

It was sort of weird being at the ocean with my dad and Pamela and Elizabeth. Dad and I are early risers, and sometimes we'd get up and go walking along the beach looking for shells before breakfast. Elizabeth usually got up around nine, and Pamela didn't get up at all unless we made her. It was Pamela, though, who wanted to stay up all night. I'd be half dead for sleep, and Pamela would decide she wanted to walk to the end of the boardwalk and back. Dad finally said we had to be in every night by eleven. Pamela wasn't too happy about it, but she was, after all, a guest.

By the fourth day, Elizabeth was getting a little annoyed at Pamela. Once, when a boy asked Pamela to go up on the boardwalk and have a Coke with him and she went, Elizabeth said, "I think it's awful the way she flirts with other boys when she's supposed to be going with Mark Stedmeister. There he is, pining away back home, and she's off drinking Cokes with some guy."

I didn't think Pamela should be going off with boys either, but I wasn't exactly sure about Mark pining away back home.

"Once you marry," Elizabeth added, "you can't even *think* about another man. In that way, I mean. It's a sin."

Elizabeth knew a lot more about religion than I did, but that really surprised me. "You can't even *think* it?" I asked.

"Not in *that* way," Elizabeth said again.

We took the inner tubes Dad had brought to the ocean and went out just beyond where the waves were breaking. Then we floated lazily around, paddling with our hands.

"*Look* at her!" Elizabeth said, pointing, when Pamela came back. Now there were two boys on the beach towel with her, and Pamela was laughing, her beautiful long yellow hair hanging down her back and touching the sand. "Pamela's going to be married and divorced by the time she's twenty," Elizabeth predicted.

I began to feel a little responsible. Here I had invited Pamela to the ocean, and she just seemed to have forgotten all about Mark Stedmeister back home. I thought about that bathing suit she was wearing, and I knew her mother had gone with her to buy it. I wondered why a mother would buy such a suit for a daughter who wasn't supposed to kiss until she was sixteen. Some parents don't seem to have a bit of sense.

The boys must have been teasing Pamela because suddenly she got up and ran along the water, the boys after her, her long blond hair flying out behind. Pamela could have been wearing a bathing suit that reached from her neck to her ankles and boys would still stare because her hair was so beautiful.

One of the boys started splashing water on Pamela's almost-bare body, and she squealed and covered her navel.

"That's disgusting," said Elizabeth.

Pamela ran up and down the beach, laughing. Then a third boy joined in, and Pamela, shrieking, turned and headed out into the water toward us just as a huge breaker came rolling in.

Elizabeth and I couldn't help but laugh when Pamela went under. It was the first time she'd gotten her suit wet since we arrived. We giggled out loud and waited for Pamela's head to come back up. The two boys were looking for her, too, and finally I saw Pamela struggling to her feet, her long hair in strings down her back. She was gasping and coughing and trying to wipe the water out of her eyes. And suddenly Elizabeth and I rose half up on our inner tubes and stared because Pamela's bikini top had slipped down around her waist, and she didn't even know it. We yelled at her, but she couldn't hear us.

The boys were staring too. Two of them grinned

and turned away, then they looked back and stared some more.

Pamela was still choking and sputtering, and not one of those boys did anything but stand there and look at her. And all at once I saw Pamela groping for her bra. She crossed her arms in front of her and sank down in the water, her face crimson. Then, with the boys laughing behind her, she dashed up out of the water, across the sand, and headed for the cottage.

Elizabeth and I were already paddling toward shore. We gathered up the towels and followed.

"Well, maybe now at least she'll settle down and stay with *us* for a change!" Elizabeth said.

She was right. When we got back, Pamela was lying face down on her bed, sobbing. She said she was going to stay right there for the rest of the week, that she wouldn't set foot outside the cottage for anything.

"Those boys don't even *know* you," I said.

"They know I'm flat-chested," she sobbed.

Dad invited us all to Phil's Crab House for dinner, but Pamela wouldn't go. We brought back a McDonald's Big Mac for her.

"C'mon, Pamela," I said the next day. "Let's at least go down to the rides at the end of the boardwalk."

"They'll *be* there! I know it!" Pamela wailed.

What happened at last was that Pamela went in disguise. She piled her long blond hair on top of her head, fastened it with a comb, put on a straw hat to cover it up, sunglasses to cover her eyes, and a long-sleeved shirt of Dad's that came down below her knees. Nobody looked at her twice, and that was just the way Pamela wanted it.

When we got home that day, Dad was sitting on the porch sipping wine with a woman. It turned out that she owned the cottage next door to the Surf and Spray Hideaway, and Dad had invited her over for a drink. We politely said hello, went on upstairs, and sat out on the second-floor porch, leaving the lower porch to them. It seemed sort of odd, staying out of Dad's way so he could have a little romance in his life.

Sitting up there with my feet on the railing, I was thinking that it's a long way from all the horsing around that boys do at the beach to the polite conversation that was going on below. It was hard for me to think of Dad ever yelling and running around on the sand like a savage, but I suppose he did.

The thing is, sometimes Patrick and Mark and Tom acted as though they were practically grown men, and the next minute they were like four-year-old kids. Sometimes we were proud to be out with them, and sometimes we were actually embarrassed. But I was still glad that the three of us had boyfriends back home and, as Dad turned some music on down below, I was thinking how lucky we were—Pamela, Elizabeth, and I—to be able to start seventh grade as couples.

11
Lester's Surprise

SOMETIMES I LOOK at Lester and wonder if he was left on our doorstep as a baby. I actually asked Dad once if Lester was related to us. What was he like as a little kid, I wanted to know. Dad said the thing about Lester was that whatever you asked him to do, he did the opposite. He said that if Mama wanted him to come in for dinner, she'd have to tell him he couldn't come in the house until bedtime, and right away he'd be banging on the back door. If she wanted him to play outside, she'd tell him he couldn't go out. The way they raised Lester, I guess, was to talk to him backward.

It's not that Lester's mean to me or anything. He just doesn't think. Or if he thinks, it's the wrong thing. Like sending Patrick upstairs right after I got a permanent. I remember the week before my eighth birthday, when Lester told me he got a really nice present for me. A bike? I wondered. A dollhouse with real chandeliers? I was trying to guess, and that's when Lester told me that it was alive. Then I was *really* excited. A pony? A dog? On the day of my birthday Lester gave me this big box and told me to open it gently. *Kittens,* I thought, because it was so quiet. You know what I found in the box? A cactus—because I'd hardly ever have to water it, he said. I cried.

"I thought it was something that *moves!*" I told Lester.

You know what he gave me for my ninth birthday to make up for it? A hermit crab. Even though I took good care of it, it only lived for about a year and then it dried up and its legs fell off. You can never tell about Lester.

So on Saturday morning at the ocean, a day before we left for home, I wasn't surprised to see Lester coming across the beach toward us. I was sitting there in my gorgeous new green and silver swimsuit with Pamela, who was trying to stick on the little metal butterflies that kept falling off her toenails and still keep on her hat and shirt and sunglasses so the boys wouldn't know who she was if they came around again. We were all listening to Elizabeth's radio and wondering what the guys were doing back home.

To tell the truth, I think we were all a little homesick. Now that we'd had a week to ourselves, we wanted to see the boys again, to be back in our own neighborhood to finish out the summer. The plan, though, was for Lester to come down Saturday and bring Crystal Harkins. She was going to sleep in the fourth bunk bed in our room, and I was secretly hoping that somehow I would get to see her big breasts. Without any clothes on, I mean. Not having a mother, I'd never really seen live breasts up close. So I wondered why Lester was there without Crystal.

Before I could open my mouth, he said, "Now, Al, don't get mad."

I squinted up at him. "Why should I be mad?"

"If you don't like the idea, I'll turn right around and drive back to Silver Spring."

"*What* idea?" I asked. That's Lester. He always talks in code.

"Just say no, and I'll take him back," Lester said. I could tell he was trying to be very, very careful, and my first thought was that Lester had brought Jimmy Benton here for me to take care of.

"Who?" I asked.

"Patrick," said Lester. "I told him to wait in the car."

"Patrick!" we all shrieked together.

"Crystal had to work. She couldn't come. So I thought maybe Patrick might like to come for one night and ride back with us tomorrow."

How is it that a brother who can buy you a cactus as a birthday present can do something so absolutely wonderful? Before I could say a word, here came Patrick, holding his shoes and socks in one hand, gingerly making his way across the hot sand.

I got up and ran to meet him. I felt like one of those women in the shampoo ads running across the meadow in slow motion to meet her lover, her beautiful hair blowing in the wind. Patrick stopped right there, the sand sticking to his feet, and stared at me.

"Gosh, Alice, you look great!" he said. And he put one arm around me and gave me a little kiss, right in front of all the boys who were watching.

That day was probably one of the nicest days of my life. After Patrick had talked with Elizabeth and Pamela awhile, he went back to the cottage to change, and then he and I went out in the water. It was really weird standing there in the water with our bare legs touching. When a breaker came in, I'd hold onto Patrick tightly, and we'd both jump up to get over it. Once, though, we were looking the other way and it turned us over, the water thrubbing in our ears, the sandy bottom scraping our elbows. Patrick had a great time.

Later, after Pamela and Elizabeth went back to the cottage, Patrick and I stayed there watching some high school kids horsing around in the water. It's a teenage game, I guess. Two boys were playing. Each got a girl to sit on his shoulders and held her legs in front. The object was to see which girl could push the other off the boy's shoulders into the water. There was always a lot of screaming when a girl fell off. I wondered if I'd ever do things like that when I was fifteen or sixteen. I liked my life just as it was that very minute —just sitting there on the sand with Patrick—our bare feet rubbing together, our arms touching, the sun warm on our backs.

That evening was fun, too. Lester went out and brought home Popeye's Fried Chicken for supper— spicy chicken, red beans and rice, butter biscuits, cole slaw, and lots of hot apple pies—so much for everyone that all six of us ate until we were stuffed, and there was still food left over.

After that Lester and Dad went bowling, and Patrick, Elizabeth, Pamela and I put on our sweatshirts and headed down the boardwalk toward the amusement park at the end. We went on the rides and took a tour through the haunted house, sitting in a coffin that went around on a track where dead bodies jumped up and wax dummies of people were being sawed in two in front of our very eyes. I screamed a lot, and Patrick kissed me. There was sure a lot of kissing that night. I would have had paper clips all over my clothes if I had lived forty years ago. Maybe I *would* be one of those girls who rode around on a boy's shoulders when I was sixteen.

When we got back, Pamela and Elizabeth went on upstairs, but Patrick and I went down to the water to walk along the beach in the dark, and then we went up and sat in the rockers on the porch, me in Patrick's lap. We didn't even hear Dad's car coming back. Dad went next door to visit the neighbor lady, and the next thing I knew, there was Lester sitting in a rocking chair beside us, his feet on the railing. He could at least have coughed or something.

I felt a little guilty about Pamela and Elizabeth that night. I mean, they were my guests, and here I was out on the porch with Patrick. Pamela had said she'd leave us alone so we could "make out." I didn't like it when Pamela talked like that.

It was two o'clock in the morning before we all went to bed. Lester and Patrick were sleeping in the front bedroom next to ours. I was so tired I just crawled in bed without a bath, but I could hear Pamela and Elizabeth giggling in the other bunks.

"What's so funny?" I asked.

"I promised not to tell," said Elizabeth, and then her voice turned serious. "But it's a sin," she added, "what Pamela's going to do."

I couldn't imagine what Pamela could possibly do to upset me and was too sleepy to care. I must have gone to sleep within two minutes.

Sometime during the night—maybe only a few minutes later, maybe an hour—I was conscious of somebody walking across the bedroom floor. I heard a door open. A floor creak. Quiet.

And then I heard a scream—a sort of squeaky squeal, actually—then footsteps again. There was Lester's voice, a screen door slamming, footsteps running, and suddenly Pamela came crashing into our room and dived into her bed.

"I *told* you!" said Elizabeth.

I raised sleepily up on one elbow. "What's going on?"

"Pamela tried to get in bed with Patrick," Elizabeth said reproachfully.

Now I was *really* awake. *"What?"*

"It was just a joke!" Pamela panted. "I was just going to surprise him and make him think it was you."

"Pamela!" I yelled. I was really getting sick of her.

"I got the wrong bed!" Pamela wailed. "It was Lester."

I didn't know whether to laugh or not. "Serves you right," I said.

"You could go to hell for that, Pamela," said Elizabeth.

The room got very quiet.

"Just for going into a boy's *room*?" Pamela asked.

"You did more than that," said Elizabeth.

"Just for crawling in a boy's bed as a joke with all my clothes on?" asked Pamela.

"You were touching," said Elizabeth.

"The minute I felt his body I knew it was Lester and I got out," Pamela said. "For heaven's sake, Elizabeth, you can touch a boy's leg without going to hell."

"I don't know. . . ." Elizabeth said doubtfully.

"Well, *I* never learned that it was a sin, so it doesn't mean me," Pamela told her.

"It doesn't matter if you learned it or not," Elizabeth argued. "It's in the Bible about going to bed with boys."

"Elizabeth, we were all lying on the beach next to Patrick," Pamela said. "What difference does it make if you're on the beach or in bed? Nothing happened!"

"It could have. It was dark in there."

Now I was getting interested in the conversation. "It could be dark on the beach, too," I suggested.

"Well, if it was dark on the beach when you were lying beside a boy, then that would be a sin," said Elizabeth.

I tried to figure it out. "So if you lie beside a boy on the beach before nine in the evening, it's okay, but after nine it's a sin?"

"Something like that," said Elizabeth.

I wondered if I was getting the proper religious instruction.

"What about you, Pamela?" I said. "How come your mother doesn't want you to kiss before you're sixteen? Is that your religion or something?"

"She just doesn't think I'm ready till then."

"Hoo boy!" I said. "Little does she know. You said she'd cut off your hair if she found out."

"Our kind of kissing doesn't count," said Pamela.

"Why not?"

"Because I hold my breath."

I sat straight up in the darkness. "What does *that* have to do with it?"

"We don't breathe each other's breath," Pamela told me.

I decided there were a lot of things I didn't know.

I wasn't sure if this was sex education, health education, or religion, but I knew I ought to give Aunt Sally a call one of these days and have a talk.

Elizabeth had just started to tell us the difference between a mortal sin and a venial sin when someone pounded on the wall next to us.

"Will you girls kindly knock it off?" Lester called. "Patrick and I want to sleep."

12
Breakup

LESTER SAID he was going to give Dad some relief and drive us all back home in his car, which made Dad happier than anything else that had happened the entire trip. Dad decided to stick around and have an early supper with the woman next door. So we put all our bags in Lester's trunk. Elizabeth and I got in the backseat with Patrick and made Pamela sit up front with Lester. Pamela was so embarrassed about what had happened the night before that she draped a beach towel over her head and sat like some veiled woman in a Spanish church all the way back to Silver Spring.

I kept thinking about what a wonderful weekend it had been. It was hard to remember that just last year I had moved to Silver Spring, started sixth grade in a new school, and been assigned to a teacher I didn't think I could like in a million years. I had felt so jealous of Elizabeth Price and Pamela Jones I could hardly stand it. And here I was, sitting in the backseat of Lester's car with a boyfriend, having looked absolutely gorgeous on the beach in a new bathing suit. Life was wonderful all of a sudden. It was unreal.

Patrick held my hand all the way home, too. He kept his other arm around me and every so often he'd lean over and we'd kiss. Elizabeth always squirmed when he did that, the way I used to squirm during the kissing scenes in movies. I tried to keep the conversation going to include Pamela and Elizabeth, but Pamela was pretending to be asleep under her red and white striped beach towel, and Elizabeth was sitting as far as she could on her end of the seat to keep her leg from touching Patrick's.

Lester drove Patrick home first because we were passing his house, then Pamela, then Elizabeth. All of us agreed that we'd meet on the playground later with Mark Stedmeister and Tom Perona and all go to High's together to celebrate being home again.

"Have a good time?" Lester asked me as we went in the house.

"Fantastic!" I said. "Thanks for bringing Patrick."

"Well, you never know about girls—what they're thinking," he said.

I almost wished I could wear my bathing suit to the playground that night to show Mark and Tom how ravishing I was in it. I considered wearing just the top, with jeans, or the bottom, with a long shirt over it, but I lost my nerve and put on shorts and a T-shirt instead. Since Dad wouldn't be home for dinner, Lester and I ate plums and cheese crackers, and I was looking forward to the ice cream at High's.

Mark Stedmeister was really glad to see Pamela. They kissed and kissed on the swings, and I remembered how Pamela was holding her breath all the while so they wouldn't breathe into each other's nostrils or whatever, and wondered just how long she could go without air. Aunt Sally told me once that when she was young, she thought you got pregnant from kissing.

We talked and kidded around for half an hour before we realized that Elizabeth and Tom Perona hadn't come yet.

"Where's Tom?" I asked Mark.

"I don't know," he said. "Haven't seen him much all week."

I looked at Pamela. "Elizabeth said she'd be here, didn't she?"

Pamela nodded. "Around seven, she said."

We waited until eight o'clock, then we all walked up the street to Elizabeth's house. Mrs. Price came to the door and said that Elizabeth wasn't feeling too well and had gone to bed early. We went to Tom Perona's next, and he wasn't there, so we went to High's without them.

Patrick was pretty tired, so we all went home about ten. Lester was watching TV and I had just gone out to the kitchen and was standing by the refrigerator with the door open when the phone rang. It was Elizabeth.

"Alice," she whispered. "Come over."

I didn't even ask what was wrong. I stuffed another cheese cracker in my mouth and ran across the street. Elizabeth was standing out on the sidewalk waiting for me, and as soon as I was within three feet of her, she started to sob.

"Elizabeth!" I said, putting one arm around her. "What's wrong?"

She sobbed even harder. She leaned her head on my shoulder and simply bawled.

"Want to sit down on your steps?" I asked.

She shook her head. "Let's walk," she said. "I don't want Mom to hear."

We walked.

"What's wrong?" I kept saying about every five seconds.

Finally, in answer, Elizabeth held out her arm. I stared at her. Had she tried to slit her wrists or something?

"What?" I kept saying.

"No ID bracelet," she cried. "T-Tom and I b-broke up. It's over."

I kept hoping it was going to be something silly like what happened between Pamela and Mark Stedmeister and the Uplift Spandex Ahh-Bra. I kept thinking that by tomorrow I'd find out that Tom had brought her a box of Whitman's chocolates and that everything was all right. I wanted us to go on the way we had been—six people, three couples, all going into seventh grade.

"Why?" I asked.

"H-H-He . . ." Elizabeth's words came out in jerky sobs. "He's g-going with somebody else."

Somebody else? Elizabeth goes to the ocean for one week and Tom Perona finds somebody else?

"Who? I hate her already!" I cried loyally.

"I don't know. S-Somebody from St. Joseph's," she wept.

We sat down on a low stone wall in front of a house, and I kept my arm around Elizabeth as though she were my little sister. Bit by bit the story came out. When Elizabeth got back from the ocean, Tom called and said he wanted to talk. When he came over, Elizabeth came out on the porch and Tom didn't even sit down. He just stood there with his hands in his pockets, staring out at the street. He said he'd been doing some thinking while she was gone, and he'd met this girl, and he thought maybe he'd like to give his ID bracelet to her, and could he please have it back.

I just couldn't believe it. How could a boy like you one week—*love* you, even—and want his bracelet back the next? Elizabeth was bawling all over my shoulder. She desperately needed someone to talk to. She couldn't tell her mother about Tom asking for his bracelet back because her mother didn't even know she had it in the first place.

Oh, man, did I ever hate Tom Perona! I even felt

a little mad at Mark Stedmeister and wondered what he had been up to while we were gone. Even Patrick! Then I remembered how Pamela had flirted with the boys at the ocean until her bra came off. It wasn't just boys who could get attracted to someone else. It was anybody. I felt sort of sick at my stomach.

"I'm going to be an outcast in seventh grade," Elizabeth said.

"Don't be ridiculous," I told her.

"If Tom didn't like me, maybe no one will," she went on.

"You're talking crazy, Elizabeth!" I said. "Besides, who said Tom doesn't like you? He just likes somebody else better." That wasn't the right thing to say.

"You know why he likes her better?" Elizabeth said after a bit.

"Why?"

"Because she lets him kiss her, and I didn't."

Now I really stared at Elizabeth. "You *didn't*? Not even once?"

She was bawling again.

"For heaven's sake, Elizabeth, what have you been doing all this time?"

"There's more to life than kissing," said Elizabeth.

"Well, sure, but . . . I mean, it's not a sin!" I said to her.

"I don't know," she said miserably. "I guess I thought that since I was going with a boy, and Mom didn't know about it, it would make it okay somehow as long as he didn't kiss me."

You know what I think? I think that people talk about being "madly in love" because they go slightly crazy. Here was Elizabeth going with a boy but not kissing, and Pamela kissing but holding her breath. Were we nutty or what?

Elizabeth slowly got to her feet, and I followed her down the sidewalk.

"Everything's going to be okay, Elizabeth. You'll have another boyfriend by Halloween, I'll bet."

I could tell by her face that Halloween seemed five years off. She shook her head. "I'm not going to have another boyfriend *ever!*"

"Elizabeth!"

"I'm thinking of becoming a sister."

"A sister?"

"A nun."

"Elizabeth!" I couldn't think of anything else to say, so I just kept saying her name.

"A nun is even better than being married," she said. "Then I won't have to worry about boyfriends again ever."

Somehow that didn't sound like a very good reason for choosing nunhood.

I wanted to say something comforting to her when we got back to her house, but her mother was standing at the screen wondering what was going on, so we just said goodnight and Elizabeth went on inside.

What happened was that I walked away from one problem and right into another. Dad had come home while I was gone, and he and Lester were facing each other across the living room. Lester had muted the sound on the TV but his eyes were still on the screen. I walked on past them and went out in the kitchen to see if the refrigerator had miraculously filled up since the last time I'd looked, but I stood just inside the kitchen door so that I could hear.

"It doesn't matter how I know," Dad was saying. "When I come home from a trip and find out that you've been entertaining women in my bedroom, Lester, I get mad as heck."

I stopped chewing. Somehow "entertaining women" didn't seem like quite the right words. Dad has a way of saying things rather quaintly. I knew that Lester certainly had not been playing his saxophone or tap dancing.

"What exactly is it that teed you off about it?" Lester asked.

"I don't like your sneaking around behind my back, waiting until I'm out of the house, and then having women in my bedroom."

"It wasn't women, Dad, it was only Crystal. And if I'd asked in advance, would you have let me?"

"No," said Dad.

"So I didn't ask," said Lester.

"You deliberately did something that you knew I would disapprove of. I don't like to feel you can't be trusted, Les."

"Look, Dad, I figured you knew already."

"Suspected, but didn't know."

"Crystal and I are pretty serious about each other."

"Not in my bedroom, you're not."

I suddenly didn't want to hear anymore. I figured that however Lester had been entertaining Crystal Harkins, he didn't deserve any more cheese crackers, so I took the whole box up to my room, sat down on the floor by my window, and ate them all.

Across the street Elizabeth was sobbing her heart out, I knew. Somewhere down the block, Tom Perona was putting his ID bracelet on another girl. Lester and Dad were discussing the details of Lester's private life. I looked at the clock. It was a few minutes after eleven. That meant it was only a little after ten in Chicago. I went to the telephone in the upstairs hallway and called Aunt Sally.

Aunt Sally said she was just getting ready for bed and had put cold cream all over her face, but it didn't make a bit of difference, I could call her anytime, and what on earth was the matter?

I told her about how we'd gone to the ocean and how Pamela had tried to crawl in bed with Patrick but got Lester instead, and I wanted to know if this was a sin, the way Elizabeth had said.

"I'm so glad you asked me that," Aunt Sally said. She always says that. I could call her at four in the morning to ask about breathing in when you kissed, and she'd still say she was glad I'd asked.

"Actually," said Aunt Sally, "a girl could get under the covers with a boy and spend the whole night and it could be an act of mercy, pure and simple."

"It *could*?" I said, getting interested.

"Let's say there was a blizzard," said Aunt Sally, "and there were this boy and girl somehow stranded in this farmhouse, and there was no wood for the fire and only one bed and one blanket. Huddling against each other there in bed would be a simple act of mercy."

"What about if there *wasn't* a blizzard?" I asked.

"It depends entirely on what's going on in your mind," said Aunt Sally.

Things were really getting complicated now.

"If a boy and a girl aren't married and a girl gets in bed with a boy with the intention of arousing him, that would be a sin," said Aunt Sally.

"Oh," I said. "Well, what if she just does it for fun, like Pamela?"

"Was she dressed?"

"All but her shoes," I said.

"Was Patrick dressed?"

"I don't know. She got Lester."

"Well, I'm just glad your father had the sense to have Lester there as a chaperone," Aunt Sally told me.

I didn't tell Aunt Sally what was going on in our living room at that very moment.

"Alice," said Aunt Sally before I hung up, "you do know how babies are made, don't you?"

"Yes," I said. "We learned that in health and hygiene back in fifth grade."

"Good," said Aunt Sally, and I could tell she was relieved. "But if there's anything else you need to know, dear, anything at all, I want you to call me."

I promised.

I went back in my room and sat down by the window again. There were love problems all around me, and it seemed only a matter of time before something happened between me and Patrick.

13
Love Letters

WE STILL HAD the first week of September to go before school started because Labor Day came late, but on Monday it rained the whole day. I was so glad it hadn't rained at the ocean while we were there, though, that I didn't care. Elizabeth was over at her house practicing to be a nun and wouldn't come outside anyway.

To tell the truth, I was pretty scared about starting junior high. Back in sixth grade, when Patrick was throwing candy bars to me while he was on the patrol duty, the closest we got to touching was a Milky Way flying through the air.

Now we were into French kissing, and Tom breaking up with Elizabeth, and Lester entertaining women in Dad's room. Somehow life seemed to be rushing ahead faster than I was ready for. I'd barely

get comfortable with one thing, and then—bam!
—something new was happening.

I thought of the way it used to be when Patrick
would just sit beside me at lunch in the all-purpose
room or come over and sit on the porch railing. Or
even the way the six of us used to walk around the
neighborhood at night after Patrick and I started kissing. Why can't good things last forever? Because, Dad
told me once, nothing stays the same, but *some* things
actually change for the better.

I wasn't so sure about that. I'll admit, I looked
pretty nice at the beach in my new bathing suit. In
some ways my body was changing for the better, but
my feet were still huge and my knees were too bony
and Lester said I had elbows like ice picks. To make
it worse, Pamela said that her New Jersey cousin told
her that knees and shoulders were "in," and if you
didn't have at least one leather skirt with a slit in it and
at least one beautiful knee to show through the slit,
you might as well wear a gunnysack to school. Boy, I'd
hate to live in New Jersey.

If I felt shaky, though, it was going to be an even
worse week for Janice Sherman, because this was *her*
week at her beach house, and not only was it raining
but she'd probably found out by now that Dad had
been visiting with her neighbor while we were there.
If Loretta Jenkins, who runs the Gift Shoppe, and Janice Sherman, in charge of sheet music, had their way,
they both would be Mrs. McKinleys. Janice would be
Mrs. Ben McKinley (he's my dad), and Loretta would

be married to Lester. Then we'd be one big musical family. Dad would play the violin, Janice would play the flute, Lester would play the guitar, Loretta would sing country music, and I'd play the triangle. Not all at the same time, though. Can you imagine what Christmas would be like at our place?

Patrick couldn't mow lawns in the rain, so he came over for a while, and I let him come in the house this time. He taught me to play the top part of "Chopsticks" on the piano while he played the bottom part. I never knew I could do it. I could actually make music that sounded good. Patrick said he had a book of easy duets at home, and he'd teach me to play some more. All I had to do was press the right keys in the right order and count how many beats to hold them down, and I did that part all right. Surprise! Music!

After he went home, though, the rain kept coming, so I went up in the attic to look for some clothes of Carol's that Aunt Sally had sent a couple of years ago. She told Dad that some of them might fit me now. He didn't remember where he'd put them, but thought they might be in the attic. I was sort of hoping I'd find an old skirt of Carol's with a slit in it.

I don't know why I hadn't spent more time in our attic. Maybe I was a little afraid of what I might find. I'd already seen pictures of myself and Mama, of course: Mama bringing me home from the hospital, Mama nursing me at her breast, Mama holding a cake in front of me on my first birthday, Mama pulling me in a wagon. . . . But looking at pictures was sort of like looking at a movie of somebody else's life. And I realized when I opened a trunk that I was probably going to find things of Mama's—things that she had touched —and I wasn't sure how I'd feel about that.

The first thing I found, actually, was a little dress that I had worn when I was two. It was in a large brown envelope that said, "Alice's dress at two years of age." It was pink, with white ruffles at the bottom and around the sleeves. And then, in another envelope, older and more wrinkled, another dress of yellow silk, and on this envelope Mama had written, "Marie's dress when she was two."

I laid them both out side by side. Mama's dress was a little larger and a little longer than mine. I thought it would be nice if some day I had a daughter and we'd keep the dress *she* wore when she was two. I folded up both dresses carefully and put them back in the envelopes.

I knew somehow that I was going to bawl when I looked in this trunk, but I didn't until I found a little brown monkey I remembered from when I was very small. And then I remembered *very* well how Mama used to fill a doll's baby bottle with water and I'd put the nipple in the monkey's mouth and after a while the water could come out his bottom. And I remembered how Mama used to make diapers out of dish towels for my monkey and help me change its diapers. That's when I started crying. I cried, too, when I found pictures I'd drawn for Mama back in nursery school, pictures she had saved. And a paper with an outline of Mama's hand traced on it and then on the inside of that, an outline of my own hand, right there with Mama's. That *really* brought the tears.

Halfway through the trunk, I realized that the clothes Aunt Sally sent wouldn't be in there at all— these were all keepsakes—but I kept going, bawling the whole time. I even went downstairs, brought up a box of Kleenex, and went on crying. It just seemed important to me somehow that I go through the trunk this summer, that before I started seventh grade with a boyfriend and everything, I really get to know all I could about my mother.

And then, down in one corner of the trunk, I found a little blue box, tied with a blue string, and it said in Mama's handwriting, "Our letters."

My heart thumped madly. It almost hurt, pounding against my chest. First I examined the string. It was tied in a bow, not a knot, so it could be opened easily. I figured that if Mama hadn't wanted anyone to read those letters, she would have at least tied a knot. In fact, she would have taped the box shut or written "personal" on top, but she hadn't.

Then I thought about Dad. These were *his* letters, too. I could always go to the phone, call the Melody Inn, and ask him if I could read them. But then I thought how if he didn't want me reading them, *he* could have written "personal" on the box, and how, if he was ever run over by a truck or something, I'd be reading the letters anyway, so it didn't seem to matter whether or not I read them now.

I lifted the lid. Those in white envelopes were postmarked Tennessee, and the ones in the blue and yellow and pink envelopes were postmarked Illinois. The letters were arranged in order; I could tell by the dates on the postmarks. One of Mama's letters came first:

Dear Ben,

You didn't think I would write, did you? I always do what I say. Just wanted you to know that it was a wonderful weekend and yes, a girl from Illinois *can* get to like a boy from Tennessee very much. I wonder if the boy from Tennessee feels the same?

Yours,

Marie

It was really weird reading that letter, thinking about my dad as "a boy from Tennessee," thinking about the feelings between the lines that weren't there on paper at all. Mama sounded pretty bold to me. I wondered what they had done together that weekend that was so wonderful, and if this was their first date.

Dad's letter was next. His was even shorter:

You want to know how a boy from Tennessee feels about a certain girl from Illinois? Can I

come up again two weeks from Sunday and
show you?

I blushed. I was actually holding in my hands a
letter that had been written by my father and held in
my mother's hands. I wondered if she had blushed,
too, when she read it. I wondered if I should read any
more, and how long it would be before I got to the
"Your lips! Your arms!" part.

It didn't take very long. Six letters later, Mom was
saying:

Ben, my dearest, I sat by the window after you
left, hugging myself with my arms, but it wasn't
the same as your arms. I wish our 'every two
weeks' was every week. But then I would wish
that every week was every day and that every
day was every night. . . .

Now I really worried about reading the rest.
Maybe I should go call Dad and get permission right
now, I thought. I remembered what he'd said to Lester
about doing things behind his back. But I thought of
how these letters would be Lester's and mine someday, so I opened the next one in the pile. It was from
Dad:

Marie. *My* Marie. I've been hearing music all
week! Strauss waltzes! Mozart sonatas! Haydn
quartets! My taste in music, since I met you,

my dearest, has turned from somber to lively!
Happy music to express the joy I feel! . . .

"Ben," Mama wrote back, "all I want, all I will ever
need to be happy, is to be in your arms forever."
    I want you. I need you. There it was, plain and
simple, and after that, there were no more letters.
    I sat on the chintz chair by the trunk, my heart
pounding. It was just as Pamela had said. First, "Your
lips! Your arms!" and then, "I want you! I need you!"
Not in those same, exact words, maybe, but it was
there.
    I carefully put all the letters back into the box in
the order in which they were written and tied it again
with the blue string. At the very bottom of the trunk,
beneath the pictures that Lester had drawn, was a
large box marked "Marie's wedding dress," but I
didn't open it. I put everything back in the trunk the
way it had been, the box of love letters in the exact
same spot where they were before. I wondered if
Lester had ever read them.
    Dad once told me that he had married Mom when
he was twenty-five and she was twenty-three. That
meant that when Mom wrote the letters, a few months
before they married, she was eleven years older than
I was right then. Sometime in the next eleven years,
I would probably reach the place where I would say,
"Your lips! Your arms!" to someone, and later, "I *want*
you! I *need* you!" It still seemed a long way off. I mean,
when you spread that out over the next eleven years,

there was a lot of time between "Your lips!" and "I *need* you!" It was comforting in a way to know that I didn't have to squeeze it all into a single summer or all into seventh grade or even do it all in high school. I could take my time.

I finally found the clothes that Aunt Sally had sent. They were in a box marked "Alice" in black magic marker and it was sitting in one corner of the attic. I think I knew it was there all the time, but I was just ready to get to know my mother a little better. Someday I'd tell Dad I'd read those letters and we could talk some more about him and Mama. But for right now I just wanted to think about her myself, beginning with the yellow dress she wore when she was two.

14
Black Matches, White Gloves

TUESDAY MORNING it was still raining. *Poor Janice Sherman,* I thought. I took a bus to the mall and saw Elizabeth and her mother buying clothes for seventh grade. While her mom paid the cashier, I said, "Elizabeth, how *are* things? You feeling any better?"

She shook her head hard. I was afraid she might start crying again right there, but then she said, "Did you go to High's last night?"

"No," I told her. "It's no fun without you." I wanted to show her just how loyal we were. I didn't mention the rain.

Elizabeth swallowed. "I think I liked it better back in sixth grade . . . before the boys . . ." She blushed a little, as though she knew she was sounding crazy, but I knew exactly what she meant.

"I feel like that sometimes," I told her. "As though I'm going to wake up some morning to find myself engaged and married and having babies and . . ."

"Let's don't talk about it," said Elizabeth, as her mother came over.

So I rode home with them, and we talked about sweaters instead. And Reeboks. And what kind of shorts to buy for gym.

I guessed I was somewhere in between Elizabeth and Pamela—not as fast as Pamela but not as uncomfortable as Elizabeth. Maybe, if I just gritted my teeth, I thought, and charged out to meet whatever was coming at me next, I could get through junior high school and dates and French kissing without worrying about them so much.

I was hoping that by afternoon, when I went to the Bentons', it would be sunny again and I could fill Jimmy's wading pool in the backyard. Sometimes he'd stay there for a long time playing with his boats and buckets, and Mrs. Benton said it was okay as long as I didn't turn my back on him for a moment. Even when the phone rang, I picked him up, wet as he was, and took him in the house with me to answer. I'd learned the hard way just what can happen when you turn your back on a little kid.

But it was still raining in the afternoon, so Jimmy and I stayed inside. I cut out paper dolls all holding hands, and Jimmy drew noses and eyes on them. Then I cut out a train, the cars connected, and Jimmy drew windows on them. We took plastic-garbage-bag ties and hooked all Jimmy's play cars and trucks together into a long train and built tunnels for them to go through. Jimmy put the Playskool nurse in the seat of the fire truck, which was the engine of our train, and carefully ran the train around and around the living room so the nurse didn't fall out once. She did bang her head on a tunnel, though, and Jimmy picked her up, kissed her forehead, and put her back in the fire engine.

That night, Patrick called and said he wanted to show his appreciation for the weekend he spent at the beach. He had it all arranged, he said; he was taking me to dinner the next day at his parents' country club. I was terrified out of my mind.

It didn't make sense, for starters, because it was actually Lester who had invited Patrick to Ocean City for the night, and Dad who had paid for our food, but I knew that when a boy invites you out to dinner, you don't ask if you can bring your dad and brother, too. So I said yes and promptly went to the bathroom and threw up. It was the words "show his appreciation" and "all arranged" and "country club" that did it. I had never been to a country club in my life. I couldn't even play golf.

"We'll pick you up at seven," Patrick had said.

We? Were his parents coming, too? Were the four of us going to have dinner together? After I threw up, I went to the phone and called Aunt Sally.

"I think that will be a wonderful growing-up experience for you, Alice," she said, "and I think that Patrick is a fine young man for inviting you."

"But what will I do? How will I act?" I bleated.

Aunt Sally explained all about country clubs and how I only had to remember five things, and I would do just fine:

1. Wear a dress and panty hose.

2. Let Patrick pull out my chair for me before sitting down at the table.

3. Don't order either the most expensive or the cheapest item on the menu, but something in between.

4. Use the fork or spoon farthest away from the plate for the first course, then the next fork or spoon for the second, and so forth.

5. Don't drink the water in the finger bowl.

As soon as I got off the phone, I wrote them all down so as not to forget. Then I ran back up to my room and opened the box of Carol's clothes, which I had put in my closet. Everything was wrinkled, and most of the clothes were still too big. I shook out each piece and held it up against me in the mirror until I found a skirt (without a slit), a blouse, and a cotton jacket that, with a little ironing, I could use. Dad usually does any pressing that needs to be done, so that night we worked up an outfit for me to wear to the country club on Wednesday. My knees were knocking already.

I was dressed an hour in advance and sat on the

sofa reciting the five things Aunt Sally said to remember. I had even put some pink pearl polish on my fingernails, and I sat with my fingers spread out over my knees so as not to chip the polish.

At five after seven, a big silver car pulled up. Patrick's parents were in the front seat. Patrick got out and came to the door.

I wondered if I had to go to the bathroom. I was *sure* I had to go to the bathroom. I opened the door for Patrick and promptly disappeared upstairs. When I came down again, I realized it was the first time I had ever seen Patrick in a suit and tie. Dad was talking with him in the living room.

"Have a good time," Dad said as we went out the door.

"You look pretty, Alice," Patrick told me.

"So do you," I said. "Handsome, I mean."

You won't believe this, but Patrick's father was standing outside the car holding the door open, just like a chauffeur. I gawked.

"Alice, this is my dad," said Patrick.

"How do you do, Alice?" said his father.

"Hi," I said, and crawled in the backseat.

The whole car smelled like Mrs. Long's perfume. She turned around and smiled at me.

"Mom, this is Alice," said Patrick.

"Alice, Patrick has talked so much about you," said his mother.

"You, too," I said, and promptly blushed. Patrick hardly ever talks about his parents.

"Really?" she said, and smiled some more. She was a beautiful woman with a thin nose and gorgeous teeth. When her husband got in the front seat again, she faced forward, and the car started off. I could feel my stomach rumbling out of nervousness, not hunger, and I put my pocketbook over my abdomen and held it close. I had forgotten about the four crackers I should have eaten.

"We've been invited to a friend's house for dinner," Patrick's dad was saying, "so we're going to drop you and Patrick off at the club, Alice, and pick you up later. I think you'll enjoy it. We always have, anyway."

"I'm sure I will," I told him. I was so glad they weren't going to stay and eat with us that I felt like leaning over the front seat and throwing my arms around Patrick's father.

"The desserts are fantastic," said Mrs. Long. "Be sure to save room for something chocolate." She sort of half turned and smiled again.

About twenty minutes later, the silver car went through the gates of the country club and up the long winding drive with the golf course on either side to the big white mansion at the top of the hill. There were lanterns along the edge of the driveway, and a man in a red coat stepped forward when the car stopped and opened the door for Mrs. Long. She explained that we were the ones who were getting out, so he closed that door and opened ours, and even held my elbow as I stepped onto the pavement.

"See you later," Patrick said to his parents, and

then we were walking up the brick sidewalk to the door where another man in a red jacket was waiting. Any moment I expected a man in a red jacket to whip it off and lay it down on the path in front of me so I could walk right over it to protect my lovely feet in my lovely shoes. In fact, with the five rules I had memorized for country club dining, I thought maybe I was going to enjoy the evening after all. I turned to Patrick and smiled. And then I realized I'd left my purse in the back seat of the car.

"My purse!" I said to Patrick. "The car!"

The Longs' car had made the turn at the end of the driveway and was starting back down toward the road. Patrick yelled and ran after it. The man in the red jacket blew his whistle. Mr. Long looked around and saw Patrick racing across the grass. He stopped the car. Patrick got my purse and came back.

"Thanks," I said, so embarrassed I hardly knew what to do. "Thank you," I said to the doorman, all the while wanting to die. I didn't know whether I was supposed to tip him or not. I only had a quarter in my purse anyway in case there was a pay toilet or something, so I just stared down at my feet and went on inside.

The nice thing about my night at the country club was that leaving my purse in the car didn't seem to make any difference. The men in the red jackets acted as though it happened every day. I'll bet they'd seen worse things than that. Aunt Sally told me once about a woman in a long dress who was invited to dinner at the White House, and while she was dancing, she felt the elastic break on her pants. When they fell down around her ankles, she just stepped out of them and walked off, leaving them there on the floor, and a butler picked them up and brought them to her all folded up and said, "Your handkerchief, Madam," and she said, "Thank you," and put them in her purse and went right on with the evening as though nothing had even happened. I could never do that in a million years.

I had never seen such a beautiful dining room. The ceiling was two stories high and there were palm trees growing in buckets, and gardenias growing in pots. The waitresses were all tall and gorgeous and dressed in black tuxedos and white gloves, just like men.

The first thing I discovered about eating with Patrick at the country club was that just about everything Aunt Sally had told me was wrong. Not wrong, actually. It just didn't help. Number one, when we got to our table, a man in a black tuxedo, not Patrick, pulled my chair out for me. Number two, there were about three forks on the left side of the plate and a couple of knives and spoons on the right side of the plate, but there was also a little spoon lying crosswise at the top of the plate, and Aunt Sally hadn't said a word about that.

It was pretty exciting, though. Our table was set for two with china dishes on mirrored place mats. If you put out your hand to pick up your fork, you saw two hands. I finally figured out that the mirrors were so that after the meal was over you could sort of lean over and look at yourself to make sure there wasn't any spinach between your teeth or anything. Next to each place mat was a little black matchbook with Patrick's name in gold on the cover. I stared. *Patrick H. Long,* it said.

"That's your name," I said.

"Yeah," said Patrick.

I stared at the matchbook again. Maybe he owned the country club! Maybe his parents owned it, and he was heir to a large fortune or something! Then Patrick explained that whenever you make a reservation for dinner, they print your name on matchbooks and put one at every place at your table. "Mom made the reservation in my name, so they put my name on the matchbooks," he said.

"But we don't smoke," I said, still staring.

"It's sort of like a souvenir," he told me.

"Oh," I said, and put my matchbook in my purse.

The waitress came back and took our wineglasses away. "Would you care for refreshments before dinner?" she asked.

"Alice?" Patrick said, and looked at me.

What were you supposed to order at a country club? The woman had just removed our wineglasses and even if we'd ordered wine, she wouldn't bring us any. Coke on the rocks? Iced tea?

"Whatever you're having," I told Patrick, and felt very proud of myself.

"Perrier with lime," said Patrick, as though he drank it every day. Maybe he *did* drink it every day. Maybe butlers tied his shoes in the morning and maids turned down his covers at night.

I felt like Cinderella at the ball. Everything that happened was a little more astonishing than what had happened just before. I had barely got over the waitresses in black tuxedos and white gloves when I noticed the glass place mats. I had scarcely got over the glass place mats than I noticed the black matchbooks with Patrick's name in gold. And no sooner had the Perrier water arrived in frosted glasses with sugared rims with a slice of lime on the side than I looked up to see another waitress in a black tuxedo coming toward me carrying a rose on a pillow.

"For you, miss," she said.

I went blank. Was I supposed to take the pillow, like on the train when they pass them around in the coach car? Was I supposed to put it behind my head? Under my feet? What did I do with the rose? I started to take the pillow, but the waitress kept a firm grip on it, so I figured it was only the rose I was supposed to have. I took the rose.

"Thank you," I said.

"You're welcome," said the waitress.

Now what? I wondered. How was I supposed to eat and hold a rose at the same time? Was I supposed to lay it across my plate like a knife? I looked at Patrick. He was smiling at me from across the table. I looked at the rose. There weren't any thorns on it. The country club must hire someone just to sit in the kitchen cutting thorns off roses to be taken on pillows to all the ladies in the dining room. Just when I was about to ask Patrick what he wanted me to do with the flower, a man in a black tuxedo came to the table carrying a little vase and set it before me. I put the rose in the vase.

"Thank you," I said to the man. And then I saw that there were little bubbles in the water in the vase. There was even Perrier water for the roses! Wait until I told Pamela and Elizabeth.

The very worst moment came when we'd finished our Perrier water at last, which, for anyone who cares to know, tastes just like tap water and costs a million dollars, and a waiter brought the menus. I remembered what Aunt Sally had said about not ordering either the most expensive thing on the menu or the cheapest, but something in between. I looked at the menu. There weren't any prices. I turned it over, thinking maybe they were on the back. There weren't any there either. I wondered if I should tell Patrick that I got a misprint—that somehow they had left my prices off. In desperation I decided that I needed my quarter more to call home than I did to go to the bathroom, so I excused myself and went to the rest room to look for a phone. There was one right there in the hallway.

The phone rang four times and nobody answered. I thought I would faint. Perhaps I could just slip out the door and keep walking. And then Dad answered. I could hear music in the background, and I remembered that Dad's friends were playing chamber music at our house that night. The music sounded friendly and comforting, and I wished that I was home right then, sitting upstairs on my bed in my pajamas.

"Dad?" I gulped.

"Al!" he said. "Where are you?"

"At the country club."

"Anything wrong?"

Somebody walked by me in the hall and I waited till he had passed before I answered.

"Al?" Dad said again, louder. "What's happened?"

"There aren't any prices on the menu," I whispered.

"What? I can't hear you."

"There aren't any prices on the menu," I said. "I don't know what to order."

"Patrick's menu has the prices," Dad said. "That's so his guests will order anything they want without having to worry about how much it costs."

"What should I do?"

"Order anything you want."

"Dad!"

"If it bothers you, just ask Patrick what he would recommend."

"Thanks," I said. I went to the rest room after that and didn't need any quarters, either.

When I got back, Patrick said, "What would you like, Alice?"

"What would you recommend?" I asked, as though I said it every day.

"The scallops are good," he said. "So is the beef burgundy. But I usually get the fried chicken."

"I'll have the fried chicken," I said.

I think that people who work in country club restaurants have to go to special schools to learn it. Every dish was brought to the table separately by somebody wearing white gloves, holding the dish with a napkin. When a waitress poured more water in my glass, she held a napkin between me and the glass so that no water would splash on me accidentally. After we'd finished our salads, a waiter brought little china cups with lemon sherbet so that we could get rid of the taste of salad oil in our mouths before we ate our fried chicken. Elizabeth would positively freak out if she had to do all this eating in front of a boy.

It was fun in a way going to the country club with Patrick, but it was a little bit awkward, too. I felt more comfortable sitting on our porch swing with him than I did there. I think I'd put my panty hose on wrong, for one thing, because one leg felt sort of twisted. And Patrick, in a suit and tie, just didn't look like the Patrick I knew. Even our conversation was different. At home, on the porch, we talked about things like would there still be an Ocean City if the polar ice caps ever melted, and what was the most slices of pizza either of us had ever eaten at one time? Here in the country club restaurant among the potted palms we talked about how wasn't it amazing that lemons grew on trees and was it raining out or not and who invented Perrier water anyway?

The desserts were things I had never had before in my life, like chocolate mousse surrounded by chocolate fudge, the menu said, and grapefruit halves with ice cream and then meringue. *This is the way the Queen of England eats every day of her life,* I thought. *Even breakfast!*

We both ordered the chocolate mousse with chocolate fudge, and Patrick used the little spoon lying crosswise at the top of the plate, so I figured that's what it was for. Sometimes you can figure things out just by watching what somebody else does. When we were through and Patrick signed the check, I took the rose out of the vase, as the waitress suggested, and we went out the French doors onto the balcony.

It wasn't raining. The air was very warm and very breezy, and my hair, which was longer now but still curly, blew back away from my face. The stars were just starting to come out, and we could hear music from the dining room. It was about the most romantic place in the world, I guess, which is why I felt so uncomfortable, and whenever I feel uncomfortable, I get silly. Suddenly I put the rose between my teeth and grinned up at Patrick, like a cow with a piece of clover. I wanted to hear Patrick laugh. I wanted it to be like it was back on my front porch.

Patrick smiled, but he didn't laugh. Gently he took the rose out of my mouth, leaned over, and kissed me, and then I was glad that he did, because he was so romantic and marvelous that I knew I would remember this moment forever.

The Longs came to pick us up about nine o'clock, and Mrs. Long asked me if we'd saved room for something chocolate. I told her we'd had the mousse, and she said, "Oh, good! That's the best thing on the menu."

The Longs talked quietly to each other in the front seat the rest of the way home, as though they didn't want to disturb whatever Patrick and I were doing in the backseat, which was sitting holding hands and wondering what to talk about next.

When we got to my house, I thanked Patrick's parents for driving us to the country club, and they waited in the car while Patrick walked me to the door. And because Dad had the porch light on for his friends, and the Longs were probably watching, Patrick didn't kiss me again but just squeezed my hand and said he hoped I'd had a good time, and I squeezed back and said it was absolutely super. Then I walked into the house grinning, past the little group of men in the living room who were playing their violins, and went upstairs to my bedroom to think about this wonderful night in which, except for leaving my purse in the car, I had not done anything incredibly stupid. I'd even used the finger bowls properly when the waitress brought them around after dinner.

I put the rose in a glass of water on my dresser and sat down to look again at the little black matchbook with Patrick's name on it in gold. When I opened my purse, however, I discovered that I had accidentally stuck my linen napkin with the country club's embroidered initials on it in my purse and had carried it home with me.

I fell back on my bed, the napkin over my face. Even alone in my room I could feel my cheeks beginning to flush. I'll bet Patrick saw me put the napkin in there. I'll bet he thought I'd never seen a cloth napkin before in my life and was taking it home to show Dad.

Lying motionless on my bed, my face hot beneath the linen napkin, the sounds of violins floating up from downstairs, I realized that I was spending an awful lot of my life worrying about what Patrick thought. What Patrick thought of my breath, my teeth, my hair, my feet, my knees, my manners . . .

I really liked him—more, probably, than he guessed—but it was time to start liking myself, too. What did *I* think? What kind of a person did *I* want to be? Something was missing here, and the something was me.

15
An Emergency Mom

THE NEXT DAY, Thursday, when teachers were in the classrooms but students didn't have to go back yet, I walked over to my old elementary school to see my sixth-grade teacher. She still had the shape of a pear and she still wore the same old green dress that she'd worn so often the year I was in her class, but when she saw me in the doorway and smiled, she was one of the most beautiful women I've ever known.

"Alice!" Mrs. Plotkin said. "How nice to see you! And look at your hair—all curly!"

I sat on top of a desk and talked as Mrs. Plotkin went about straightening her desk drawers. I told her about my summer with Patrick, and she told me about her summer with Ned, her husband, and I said I was going to miss her when I was in the seventh grade.

"Well, the good thing about missing someone," Mrs. Plotkin said, "is that you've got somebody to miss. Think of all those friends you're going to make in junior high school, Alice—people you don't even know yet."

That was sort of nice when I thought about it, except that I'd rather have the people I like around me all the time and never have to miss them at all. And as for the friends I hadn't even made yet, well, there was no guarantee. Even if I had beautiful shoulders and knees and a leather skirt with a slit up the side, there weren't any promises I'd never be lonely again, were there?

Elizabeth came over after I got back, though, to show me the stuff her mom had bought her for school, and I was glad she was finally getting over Tom Perona. Even if you *were* lonely sometimes, I guess, you could get over it. As for Pamela and Mark Stedmeister, they seemed even crazier about each other than they were before. Mark had given Pamela some sort of ring (I think it was his brother's old class ring, actually), and Pamela wrapped a big wad of tape around the back of it to keep it on.

It was my last day at the Bentons', because Mrs. Benton would have to hire someone else now that school was starting. I felt really good about how much I'd helped Jimmy. That's the way mothers feel, I guess, about preparing their kids for life.

I'd been thinking a lot about mothers that summer and how I didn't have one, probably because I realized how much I wanted one. And three days before school began, I needed one in the worst way.

I woke up that morning with a headache and a stomachache both. The minute I tried to get out of bed, I threw up. All over my bedspread, all over the floor. Dad had already left for work, and I could hear Lester's car backing down the drive. When I got a towel to mop up, I vomited all over again. Yech! How did mothers ever *stand* it? What if you had seven children and they were all sick at the same time?

I rinsed out my mouth and wobbled downstairs in my pajamas to get a bucket. I wondered whether I should call Dad. Then I remembered that it was Friday morning, and Dad always had staff meetings on Fridays. I wanted to know if I should put a hot water bottle or an ice bag on my stomach. I wanted to ask if we even *had* a hot water bottle or an ice bag. I couldn't remember the last time I was so sick. I didn't think I should bother him, though, at least until the meeting was over. And much as I loved Mrs. Plotkin, I wasn't about to call the grade school and tell her I was sick.

Somehow I managed to fill a pail with water and find some old rags and go upstairs and clean up my floor. I went back down again, cleaned up the towel and the pail, drank a little milk, and was wondering if I should make some toast when the doorbell rang.

Not Patrick, I prayed. *Please, please, not Patrick!* I weaved down the hall and peeked out the curtain.

It was Mrs. Eggleston from next door. I opened the door just a little.

"Alice, I hope I didn't wake you," she said, "but the mailman left a letter for Lester in our box by mistake."

The room was beginning to whirl. I shouldn't have drunk the milk. My throat tightened as I reached for the envelope. "I'm . . . I'm sick," I said, and promptly threw up all over Lester's letter.

The next thing I knew I was on the sofa and Mrs. Eggleston had a cold wet towel on my forehead. She was gently wiping my face with a washcloth.

The fact was, I hardly even knew Mrs. Eggleston. I'd say hello to her when she was out raking her yard, and I talked to her once when her poodle got loose and I helped catch it. She'd be out on her porch reading the newspaper sometimes when Patrick and I were in the swing, but she was just an ordinary neighbor who, in a space of ten seconds or so, had become my emergency mom.

She said she wasn't going to give me any aspirin unless my dad said it was okay, but she took my temperature (102 degrees) and gave me a glass of cracked ice to chew, and then I went to sleep and when I woke up again it was about two in the afternoon and she was sitting beside the couch holding a glass of orange juice.

"We'll just wait till you feel like taking a few sips, Alice," she said.

I could tell from the smell of Pinesol that she had

cleaned up my mess by the front door. I could even see Lester's letter, cleaned and dry, propped up on the bookcase. This was truly amazing. There were substitute mothers everywhere! Mrs. Plotkin was one; Lester's old girlfriend, Marilyn, was another; Lester's new girlfriend, Crystal Harkins; Aunt Sally; my cousin Carol . . . ! Lying there on the couch waiting for my stomach to settle, I felt that there must be a mother deep inside of every woman just waiting to come out. Maybe there was even a little bit of a mother inside of me, and I didn't even have a model!

I drank some of the orange juice, and Mrs. Eggleston helped me back upstairs. She got out some clean pajamas and I could tell that she had already washed and dried my bedspread.

I let her dress me. I let her brush my hair. I let her tuck me back in bed just as though I was two years old. I didn't even care. I slept.

When I woke again, Dad was sitting by the bed holding the thermometer.

"Open up, Al," he said, and slipped the thermometer under my tongue. "Mrs. Eggleston said you were one sick girl today. Feeling any better?"

"Um hmm," I said, letting my eyes close again.

"Does anything hurt? Your neck? Your throat? Your ears?"

Why do fathers *do* that? They're just like dentists. They wait until you've got something in your mouth and then they ask you questions.

"Huh uh," I said.

Dad took the thermometer out. "Well, it's gone down a degree. That's good news. You feel like any dinner?"

"Just orange juice," I said. "And, Dad, . . . *don't* let Patrick up here."

"I won't," Dad said. "He's already called, and I told him you were sick. He said he'd phone again tomorrow."

Good old Dad. Just like he'd bought me that bathing suit at the ocean, he'd taken charge again, and everything was under control. He started to get up to go downstairs, but suddenly I reached out and stopped him.

"Dad . . ."

He sat back down. "Yeah?"

"I just wanted to tell you . . . I wanted you to know . . . well, I guess I should have asked first."

Dad looked puzzled.

"I *know* I should have asked," I said miserably. "But . . . when I was looking for those clothes of Carol's that Aunt Sally sent, I opened the trunk and found—" I turned my face away. I was too embarrassed to look Dad in the eye. ". . . I found your letters to Mom."

The room was so quiet I wondered if Dad was still there. I couldn't even hear him breathing.

"And you read them." He was there, all right.

I nodded. If the temperature in my mouth was 101 degrees, it was 110 degrees on my face. I wished Dad would say something. Anything. The silence was awful.

Finally, quietly, he said, "It's been a long time since I read those letters myself, Al. I can understand you'd be curious."

I nodded again.

"Well," he said, and without even looking at him, I could tell that he was smiling. "Did you find out anything new about your mother and me?"

"Only how much you loved each other."

Dad sighed. "We did, Al. A lot. Maybe one of these days I'll go up to the attic and read them myself. But you're right. You should have asked."

"I won't do it again. I mean, I don't open your mail or anything."

"You'd better not!" said Dad, and gave me a tap on the head.

This was Lester's night to work late at the Maytag store, so Dad fixed a Stouffer's dinner for himself and carried the portable TV up to my bedroom so I could watch. About nine, though, I turned it off and was just starting to drift into sleep when I saw Lester standing in the doorway of my room, silhouetted against the hall light. He was holding an envelope. "Where'd this come from, Al?" he said.

"I'm sorry I puked on it," I told him.

"Where did you *get* it?"

"Mrs. Eggleston had it."

"What?"

"The mailman left it there by mistake. She brought it over."

"When?"

"This *morning,* Lester! When I was sick. We cleaned it up the best we could. What's the big deal?"

Lester just turned and walked away.

I lay there looking at the empty space in the doorway where Lester had been. I remembered now that the envelope was postmarked "Bethesda," and that's where Lester's old girlfriend lived. I really liked Marilyn—maybe even more than I liked Crystal Harkins. I was here the evening they broke up with each other, when Marilyn told Lester that "it just won't work." That was all I heard, but I'd never seen Lester so sad and upset.

I got out of bed finally and went to the bathroom to get a drink. Lester was sitting at the top of the stairs, leaning against the wall, holding Marilyn's letter in his hands. When I came out of the bathroom, he was still there, so I sat down on the floor across from him.

"Don't worry," I told him. "I'm through throwing up now."

He just looked at me.

"It's from Marilyn, isn't it?"

Lester sighed. "Yeah," he said. "It's from Marilyn."

I leaned against the opposite wall. It seemed as though we sat there for ten whole minutes just being quiet together, and Lester didn't even tell me to get out of his life.

"What did she say?" I asked finally. "I mean, the parts you can tell."

Lester just looked at me again blankly, as though he were trying to figure out who I was.

"Alice," I told him.

He went on staring. "She wants to start seeing me again," he said at last.

"Whew!" I sucked in my breath.

About a year ago, Lester was grieving because Marilyn had just broken up with him and he didn't have any girl at all. Now he was grieving because he had two. I decided right then that love is about the most mixed-up thing that can possibly happen to you, and we sat there a long time together—Lester thinking about Marilyn, me thinking about Patrick.

16
Patrick and Me

"WELL," DAD SAID to me on the last day of vacation, "how was The Summer of the First Boyfriend?"

"It's not over yet," was what I told him.

It was a fateful last day. I went shopping with Elizabeth for some socks, and she told me that she was devoting her entire seventh grade to her studies and hoped to make all A's. She was going to work so hard, she told me, that she wouldn't even think about boys once.

"They mess up your life," she said.

The next thing that happened was that Pamela told me that her mother had caught her and Mark Stedmeister kissing ("*That* kind of kissing," Pamela told me, whatever kind that was). Mrs. Jones didn't cut off Pamela's hair, but she told her she couldn't go with

Mark anymore, and she had to be in the house by nine every night from now until Christmas.

There must be something about last days of vacation, because Lester had gone over to Bethesda the night before to see Marilyn and she'd said she hadn't known how much she cared about him until she'd let him go. I suppose she said a lot of other things, too (like "I *want* you! I *need* you!"), but that was all Lester told me. I never saw him look so happy, and I knew that however much he might like Crystal Harkins and her clarinet, he loved Marilyn even more. So I was happy for Lester and happy for Marilyn and sad for Crystal Harkins.

I'd been thinking about Patrick a lot the past few days. Thinking about myself, too. That's why, when Patrick came over that afternoon, I felt sort of strange inside. We sat on the porch swing and held hands, talking about Mark and Pamela and Elizabeth and Tom and Lester and Marilyn and Crystal. Patrick said that Tom had already broken up with the girl he left Elizabeth for and was going with somebody else from St. Joseph's, and that Mark Stedmeister was trying out for the basketball team and wouldn't have time to date anybody.

Every so often Patrick stopped talking and leaned over to kiss me, and I was thinking about how things used to be when Patrick would sit on the porch railing and I'd sit on the steps—not even touching yet—and he'd tell me about living in Germany and Japan and how his family used to eat squid, and then I'd tell him what it was like to sleep overnight on a train when I went to Chicago to visit Aunt Sally.

And you know something? I missed that—just being friends. I decided I needed times like that more than I needed to start seventh grade with a boyfriend. All the boys who just wanted to be friends with me would figure they had to be "boyfriends" instead, and I wouldn't even be able to go anywhere with a boy without holding hands and wiping the sweat off every chance I got. But when I thought of saying that to Patrick, my stomach flipped over. Finally, though, the words came out.

"Patrick," I said, staring down at my knees, "I really like you a lot—more than any other boy—but I just want us to be friends for a while."

Patrick got so quiet that I realized finally I was the only one pushing my feet against the floor, the only one moving the swing. His hand sort of went dead on top of my hand, and I felt scared and hollow inside. What was I *doing*?

"How come?" Patrick asked finally.

"Because I think I liked it better the way we were before," I told him. "I mean, I like this, too, but I need some more of that first. You know what I mean?"

"No," said Patrick.

I swallowed and gently pulled my hand away from his. I was probably making a terrible mistake. "There's so much *worry* and everything, Patrick. About what you think of me, I mean. About what we're going to do next. I want to like you without having to worry all the time."

"I didn't know you did," he said. That's just like a boy, not to even notice. But there was something about the way he said it that told me I wasn't the only one who worried; I was just the one who said it first.

Patrick was quiet for a minute. "I'll bet it's because of what happened to Pamela and Elizabeth," he said finally. "I'll bet that's why you want to break up."

Break up! It was the most terrifying word I'd ever heard.

"No," I said, and my voice was shaky. "Well, maybe. Partly, anyway. I just don't like to think of us getting to the place where we never speak to each other again, or where I have to be in every night by nine o'clock from now till Christmas."

"I don't either," said Patrick. "But I don't want to be just friends."

He hadn't actually moved away from me on the swing, but it seemed as though we were sitting about as far apart as we could get. As though walls had come between us. What he was saying, I guess, was that I had to choose to either go with him or we couldn't be friends at all. The scared, hollow feeling grew bigger inside my chest.

"What about being *special* friends?" Patrick said.

I looked over at him. "What's that?"

He shrugged. "Just *special.* We won't be going

with each other, exactly, but we're more than just friends. Sort of in-between."

"Do you mean that, Patrick?"

"Of course."

"You're not mad?"

He shrugged. "A little, maybe. But I'll get over it."

I wasn't sure I wanted him to get over it. I wasn't even sure what I wanted. Patrick pining away for me in his room? Patrick refusing to eat, wasting away out of love? No, I wanted us to be special friends, just as he said. But after he left, I ran upstairs and bawled.

The thing about being twelve is that you bawl a lot. I wasn't even sad, particularly. Relieved, maybe. I cried because I really do like Patrick, and hadn't meant to hurt his feelings; cried because it was over, and I wasn't sure what would happen next.

We had a gourmet meal at our house that night —pork chops and applesauce—the closest we get to gourmet. Lester fries onions in a skillet, then Dad adds some pork chops and fries those with the onions, and finally I open a can of applesauce and dump it over the top.

When we sat down at the table, Lester announced that he and Marilyn were back together.

"Well!" said Dad, and went on chewing for a while. "How is Crystal going to take it?"

"I don't know," Lester said. "I've got to tell her tonight. But I know I'm doing the right thing. It just feels right—Marilyn and me together again."

"Must be something in the air," said Dad. "I got a letter from the woman who owns the beach house next to Janice's at Ocean City. She wonders if we can't get together sometime this fall—go to a concert or something. I'm thinking about it."

"Well, Patrick and I broke up," I said, and flopped my pork chop over to see if there were any onions hiding on the other side.

"Oh?" said Dad.

"Why?" asked Lester.

I shrugged. "We decided to be special friends instead."

"Well, that sounds nice, too," said Dad.

"I don't know," I told him.

That night, after I'd gone to bed, I thought about how I'd always wondered what it would be like to have a boyfriend in winter. Somebody to snuggle up with in front of a fire. If we had a fireplace, that is. Or a boyfriend to walk with in the snow. One minute I was thinking how sad I would be not to have a boyfriend at Christmastime, and the next minute I was thinking how relieved I was that I wouldn't have to worry about what to give Patrick. And then I started crying again. Between the sixth and seventh grades, something happens to your eyes. They water a lot. I think it's so you can get all the watering out of the way before you begin wearing mascara.

The first day of seventh grade was a lot different than Pamela, Elizabeth, and I had planned all summer.

At least a half dozen times we had talked about how Mark and Patrick would come down to our bus stop and we'd all get on together and sit in pairs, but we'd be sure to talk to Elizabeth and tell everyone that she had a boyfriend at St. Joseph's.

Now it was Elizabeth and Pamela and me together, without the boys, standing there in our new Levis with sweaters sort of draped around our necks, and none of us looking especially happy. When I told Elizabeth and Pamela that Patrick and I weren't a couple any longer, they thought I was nuts; but deep down I think they were glad about it, just for the company.

"I wanted things to be like before," I said, not expecting them to understand. Elizabeth did, but Pamela didn't.

There were a lot of new faces on the bus—kids from other schools, all going to the same junior high school now. Pamela and Elizabeth slid into one of the seats, so I was odd man out. I sat down alone in the seat in front of them and stared out the window.

Five blocks farther on, the bus stopped at Patrick's corner, and there he was, his book bag slung over one shoulder. He got on, and Pamela poked me from behind. Patrick came down the aisle looking at the kids on one side of the aisle, then on the other. I wondered if Patrick—the world traveler, who could count in Japanese—ever felt odd and out of place.

Then he saw me, and I gulped. Would he snub me and just walk on by?

He didn't. Patrick stopped when he got to my seat. "Okay if I sit here?" he asked.

"Sure," I told him.

It was just like it used to be. We talked about all the new people we didn't know, and how if you missed the bus you had to take a cab or something, and how our homerooms were right next to each other.

As more people got on and the bus grew noisier and I was sure that Pamela and Elizabeth couldn't hear what we were saying, I asked, "Patrick, did you *really* mean what you said about being special friends?"

"Of course," he told me.

"It's not the same as engaged to be engaged to be married or anything?" I wanted to make sure. "I mean, it's not engaged to be engaged to going steady?"

Patrick shook his head. "It's just really special friends."

"How special?" I wanted to know.

"We can still go places together sometimes," he said. "If you want to," he added.

"I'd like that," I told him.

"But we can go out with other kids, too," said Patrick.

"Other kids" meant other girls. A sort of sad feeling filled my chest. I really didn't like to think about Patrick going out with other girls, and I wondered all over again if I'd done the right thing—if I'd given up something wonderful just because I wasn't ready for it yet. When *would* I be ready? I wondered. When I was eighteen? Twenty-six? Fifty-nine? Never? By then Patrick would be married to somebody else!

I think maybe Patrick was wondering the same thing because he said to me, "You know what? Let's make a promise that wherever we are on your twenty-first birthday, I'll call and make a date for New Year's Eve."

I stared. "What?"

"Everyone goes out on New Year's Eve once they're twenty-one," Patrick said. "My folks always go out to celebrate."

"What if you're already married?" I asked him.

"What if *you're* married?" he said in answer.

"At twenty-one?" I croaked. "Patrick, I'll barely even be grown!"

"Well, I'll call you up and find out," he said, and smiled at me. He looked just like he did that day back in sixth grade when he was on patrol duty at the corner and tossed a candy bar over to me—when I first found out he liked me.

"Okay," I said, grinning back. "I'll expect a call on my twenty-first birthday, wherever I am, which will probably be at the Melody Inn, a clerk or something dumb."

"Life is full of surprises," Patrick said. "Know who said that?"

"Somebody famous?"

"No. My mom."

The bus pulled up in the circular drive of the

school. The building was a lot bigger than our grade school. Here we would have a different teacher for each class and we'd even have to take showers after P.E. It was going to be a whole new world, and I thought how scary it was to go in there alone when I could have had a boyfriend to walk me to class.

We lined up to get out of the bus. Like a chimpanzee, Patrick had crawled over the seat to be with some boys at the back, so Elizabeth and Pamela and I squeezed out the door together.

"What did he *say*?" Elizabeth asked. "He actually had the nerve to sit with you!"

"Elizabeth, we're *friends*!" I told her. "*Special* friends. We're not mad or anything."

"Well, I think you're nuts!" Pamela told me. "You could have held hands in the halls and everything. You blew it, Alice!"

We went in different directions once we got inside the school. Elizabeth went up to second floor, Pamela turned at the corner, while I went straight ahead. I was being mangled by knees and shoulders and elbows. Wherever I looked, human bodies were coming at me, and I pressed myself against a drinking fountain to get out of the way. The water came on accidentally and made a big wet spot on the back of my shirt.

A bell rang, and the bodies came even faster. I tried to study the little map I'd gotten in the mail. There had been an orientation day for new students the week that Elizabeth, Pamela, and I were at the ocean, so we didn't get a tour of the school ahead of time like the other seventh graders did. I turned down the second corridor. What did the bell mean? Was I late already? Should I skip homeroom and go directly to my next class? Where *was* my next class? Where in the world was my locker?

I heard footsteps behind me.

"We're right at the end of this hall, Alice," Patrick said, charging on by.

It really was like old times with Patrick and me, and even better than sixth grade because we were special now. I'll bet I was the only girl in the whole seventh grade—the whole school, in fact, the whole *world,* maybe—who had a date for New Year's Eve nine years off.

I saw Patrick pause in a doorway further down. "Hey, Alice!" he called. "Catch!"

Something came sailing at me through the air and I put out my hands: a Three Musketeers candy bar, in its shiny wrapper.

"See you in the cafeteria, maybe?" Patrick said, smiling.

"I'll save you a seat," I told him, and opened the door to my room.